THE GRID 1

FALL OF JUSTICE

PAUL TEAGUE

CHAPTER ONE

Execution

Jay realized that it was all over for him.

Despite being out of breath, wet from the sweat of physical exertion, and with adrenaline levels electrifying his entire body, his survival instinct was replaced in a moment by the acceptance of certain death. These events were being watched by thousands on the big screens placed around The City. Nobody had ever achieved so much in their quest for justice. He'd lost seven of his fellow detainees along the way, all killed in terrible ways by a predator who took their lives from the safety of a computer console.

It had taken nine days to get this far. Every minute had become a struggle for survival, with traps, deceptions and hazards at every turn. Each move had been watched by the viewing public – just a small crowd at first – as the weakest were picked off, one at a time.

Soon, though, a buzz spread through The City – there was a strong leader in this challenge, and it seemed as if somebody might walk out alive. Unknown to Jay, he'd become a celebrity, with half of the population gunning for his success even though they knew that statistically it was unlikely to happen. He was the underdog in these events, but he was fighting back, fierce and defiant.

For a day or two they supposed that he might make it and win a small victory for all of them. It had only ever happened once before in the entire history of Fortrillium, but it meant that there was always a chance, the slightest possibility that there might be a victor. Jay himself had even believed for a few hours that he might make it through.

He'd seen three of the other prisoners perish by his side – one of them he'd known personally. She'd died in his arms, her body pierced in twenty places by the metal shards that had been unleashed from a hidden trap. Her name was Rina – they'd met each other on and off since childhood. As he'd felt the last embers of her life fade away through her limp body, Jay had experienced a new surge of determination, an anger and commitment to see this fight through to the end.

He was seeking justice, and this was the only way it could be done. To avoid a life rotting away in the wet cells beneath the river, incarcerated without trial, he'd have to take his chances in The Grid. It was the only way he was ever getting out.

In those final moments, with fewer than fifty minutes to survive until The Justice Walk, events had taken another turn. It was as if the person who was playing against him had been substituted: a last-minute and unannounced switch of opponent to put a stop to this challenger who dared to think that he might escape with his life.

Jay was tired and weak, but he could have fought and won against his original adversary. He'd even grown to know whoever it was well over those nine days. His opponent had a preference for traps – Jay had realized that early on in the trial, and when a life was taken it would be done dramatically. Jay knew that there were cameras all over, recording every moment for the screens, so he understood why this Gridder went for climactic deaths. It played well to the audience, whether they were gunning for the Justice Seekers or not. A tragic death on screen made the viewing figures soar and took the thoughts of those in The Climbs away from their miserable lives.

Well, they were about to get their final dramatic demise, and this time it was going to be Jay who they watched as he perished in front of them.

He felt the metal plates jolt against his body and the pressure began to build as they started to push against his back and chest. They were moving deliberately – whoever had contrived this death for him had a sense of the dramatic and a love of the horrific. He was going to have the life slowly squeezed out of him in front of an audience of hundreds of thousands. They wouldn't make it fast, they'd show every horrible moment.

Jay was finding it hard to breathe. He turned his head sideways to remove some of the pressure, even though it was only a matter of time now. He felt the sudden rise of fear, but like the wildebeest in the lion's jaws he quickly calmed and awaited the end.

In his final seconds of life he wondered how it had ever come to this. He'd been entirely innocent, as had his fellow inmates. All evidence against them was a complete fabrication; everybody knew this, yet nobody did anything to challenge it. They were powerless. His only way out had been to take on The Grid, but all detainees knew that would inevitably end with death.

For Jay, like hundreds of others before him, the scales of

justice had been leaned on, tipping them in favour of Fortrillium. As Jay's life was extinguished, watched by a horrified yet paralysed audience, he would never know how close he was to discovering the secret that they all sought. He was seconds away from the final solution, but if he'd been permitted to get any further the entire veil of deceit would have been swept away.

The two metal plates closed together, and the audience turned away from the screens, barely daring to imagine what Jay must have experienced in those last seconds. Citizens with a conscience felt a sickness deep in their stomachs; it was the bile of passive acquiescence. They all understood what had happened here. This wasn't justice. It was a public execution.

Breached

Joe Parsons forced the unruly cluster of wires into the makeshift socket and fired up his screen.

'Damn it!' he cursed, as the device flickered for a moment then faded away.

'Here, let me try something,' offered Lucy, keeping her voice to a whisper, even though there was no chance that anybody would be able to hear them down there.

Everyone was watching the screens after all. The entire city had been electrified by the way Jay had fought so hard to win his right to speak before the Law Lords. Joe and Lucy didn't know him personally, but they knew his story well enough. It's why they were down in the sewers at that moment, trying to break into Fortrillium's data centre.

A rat scuttled by Joe's foot. He flinched and kicked out as it passed by. He'd never got used to the rats. They were everywhere in The Climbs, but where Lucy lived they didn't have to put up with them. He'd grown up with them, in his bedroom and the eating areas – if they were lucky enough to have sufficient food for the vermin to steal.

She always impressed him the way the rats didn't bother her. She'd had a privileged life over on Silk Road, but you'd never have known that from the way she was with him.

Lucy stamped on the creature, her heavy boot holding it down in the stinking waters of the sewer until it stopped struggling and died. She lifted her foot and the foul corpse floated away. Another death. Like life, it was easy come, easy go, but she wasn't that casual about killing, even if it was a disgusting, diseased thing. She knew what Joe was like with rats around and she needed him focused.

She'd asked Mitchell to try and keep the pipe-way clear if he could. The last thing they wanted was Joe getting spooked again and abandoning the project halfway. He knew the risks, of course, and they all understood why he was so jittery. Only six years ago Joe's dad had suffered a similar fate to the one which undoubtedly faced Jay on that night. He was the only person keeping his mother alive. They'd been thrown into poverty since his father's death. He desperately needed to continue his dad's work, but he couldn't risk leaving his mum on her own.

'Mitchell!' Lucy hissed up the pipe-way. 'Stay alert!'

'Something is going on up there,' came the reply. 'It must be near the end now – you'll need to hurry.'

Joe teased the wires one more time. These opportunities only came along every once in a while, and if they couldn't get proof on that day, who knew how long they'd have to wait? The screen lit up. Lucy felt him relax.

'Get Wiz up here,' said Joe. 'Bring the codes.'

A lanky, skinny form worked its way awkwardly up the

pipeline, stumbling into the stinking water several times. They kept Wiz away from the action as much as they could – he was so tall he had real trouble getting along the pipes. But like so many of the teenagers living in The Climbs, he'd learned some technical skills that were immensely valuable on the black market. It was a useful set of competencies that enabled him and his friends to stay alive.

Joe and Wiz were formidable together, and with Lucy's connections and access to Silk Road there was little that they couldn't achieve between them. Except perhaps this, their biggest challenge. It was fine earning food tokens by fixing people's battered old tech on the black market, but breaking into Fortrillium was an entirely different problem.

'It's happening,' said Lucy. 'Go faster ...'

'Got it!'

Joe took the codes that Wiz had just handed him and tapped them swiftly into the interface. The console looked as if it had seen much better days. Mitchell shouted along the pipes, as loud as he dared.

'I can hear the groans outside. They must be finishing it soon.'

'Just a few more seconds ...'

Joe typed furiously at the keypad. His screen burst into life, and a stream of indecipherable data began to flow - there seemed to be pages and pages of it.

'It's true.' Wiz was relieved. 'They switched over at the last minute, there was external interference.'

'That information is coming from outside Fortrillium,' Joe continued. 'There's got to be something else out there.'

Lucy, Joe and Wiz peered at each other, huddled together and crouched in the stinking water of the sewer pipe. Lit only by the glare from the screen, they'd just got the proof they needed to confirm what Joe's dad had thought all along. When Jay had got close to the centre of The Grid, the final destination, something – or someone – had intervened.

Within moments of attaining his goal – The Justice Walk – and a chance to prove his innocence at last, Jay was deprived of his victory. Having almost beaten his opponent in The Grid, a last-minute switch was made and the rules of engagement changed right at the end of the challenge. There was no doubt about it. There was no rectitude in Fortrillium. They were sending detainees to the slaughter.

Forbidden

Talya Slater always felt guilty the moment she crossed over into The Climbs. She was one of the privileged few, for she had wealth, resources, and even some degree of influence and power. However, walking confidently through the security barriers that marked the limits of Silk Road, she did not feel that fearlessness inside.

Every time she stepped into The Climbs, she questioned her advantages in life and if it was right to hang onto them as she did. She had Lucy to safeguard; she couldn't just abandon them both to a life of poverty on a principle and a whim. She'd rationalized this to herself many times before – the best way she could help was to continue to do pro bono work, and she would be no use to anybody without her present standing in society.

She was viewed as a bit of an anomaly on Silk Road. Most people in her position would have happily helped themselves to the spoils of the misbehaving rich and feathered their nests. But Talya had always had a conscience. For as long as there was so much injustice she would continue to do her best to fight it. She did this by spending the one day that she didn't have to work helping the miserable souls in The Climbs.

The transition from Silk Road was almost immediate as she stepped through the security barrier. A massive solid concrete wall ran all around the vast boundary of Silk Road, keeping the inhabitants of The Climbs locked in – or the Silk Roaders out, who knew? Hundreds of thousands of affluent households formed a perimeter around which the residents of The Climbs were squeezed in like caged animals. There were over three million in there, piled high in decaying tower blocks that had been prosperous business centres in the days before the plague.

On the Silk Road side, the walls were fitted with projections of rural scenes; the lovely greenery never seemed to end, and the gigantic, crumbling towers of The Climbs were out of sight. Beyond the blockades, though, the truth was hard to bear, which is why so few of the rich residents ever bothered to venture inside from their affluent perimeter.

Most found it distasteful, a glimpse of a terrible world which they knew might befall them on any day. The rules of Fortrillium were strict and merciless, enforced by the menacing Centuria, a state-run team of military police who carried out the will of the Law Lords and Damien Hunter without mercy. The Silk Roaders knew never to force the issue. It was a working harmony of rich and poor, a balanced ecosystem that had ultimately saved all of their lives after the plague years. Sure, they all had a feeling of what life must be like beyond those walls, but because they weren't forced to confront the vast concrete barriers which separated them, it was easy to forget. It was even more convenient to deny what was going on.

Talya was a different beast, but she was also a clever one. She knew enough to understand that if she chose the wrong battles she too would end up incarcerated. She would be another victim of the Centuria. There would be a mysterious late-night visit from their threatening mob and a series of allegations that seemed unlikely to most people. The only way to resist this was through influence and power, by using her lucky advantage to move closer to the centre to try to change things that way.

Six days of the week she spent her time sorting out the trivial affairs of the wealthy, attending to relationship break-downs, property concerns, legal contracts and financial matters. On Sundays she walked among the high towers of The Climbs. They were known as The Climbs because the elevators that served them had long since broken down. The only way to access the upper levels was via the crumbling stairways that formerly acted as fire escapes, in the days before the plague came. It had been well before her memories began – she was too young to remember any of it.

There was only one resident that she knew of who could recall what had happened when the change came. There must have been others, but they were old and life was harsh. That person was Harry – Harriet – a 103-year-old inhabitant of the tower that Talya was standing in front of at that precise moment. She lived on the thirty-third floor, so at her age and with her frailty she'd been just like a prisoner there for many years.

She steeled herself for the long climb but knew that it would be worth it when she got up there. She'd finally coaxed Harry into sharing with her the truth about what had happened during the years of the plague.

CHAPTER TWO

Prey

Damien Hunter stared out from his office window, intermittently surveying the reports that were laid out in front of him on the dark wooden desk. These were updates filed by the Centuria, the latest batch of inhabitants who'd aroused suspicion or challenged the dominance of Fortrillium in some way.

With a population getting close to four million in The City, it took fifty teams of military personnel to manage the trickier intelligence elements of policing, working alongside the regular law enforcement units.

It never ceased to amaze him. Even though they'd created a societal system in which hundreds of thousands flourished, albeit at the expense of many others who were forced to do the physical work, there was always resistance from the privileged. Why couldn't they just shut up and enjoy their lives of advantage?

The equilibrium within this sanctuary was perfect, so long as nobody made waves. A minority of the wealthy and favoured profited from a majority of the poor and deprived. It was always that way, whichever political system you chose to adopt. There were winners and losers in capitalism; the same was true for communism or any other form of governance that had been used to run a country. There were always going to be winners and losers.

The impoverished would seldom be denied access to food or shelter, that's when riots and mob resistance became a threat. They'd have to work for provisions of course. That's why he'd continued to support the Centuria, to maintain that perfect balance between rich and poor. Within those groups, you always had dissenters and lawbreakers.

The lawbreakers were easy, they were all sent to The Soak. The Soak was a vast underground prison, so-named because it had been located under a river. It housed several thousand lawbreakers in over-packed cells and once incarcerated there your only chance of escape was to seek justice in The Grid. The watercourse itself lay beyond The City's boundaries. It could not be accessed from inside the walls, and it was imperative for order and discipline that nobody ever saw the outlying area from above ground. The Soak solved most of his problems with city discipline.

It was all a matter of stability. Monitoring population growth and depletion, putting an immediate stop to any form of lawbreaking or resistance, maintaining the perfect economic balance between rich and poor: someone had to do the work after all. Every societal model in history had relied on a manipulated majority who aspired to little more than sustenance and shelter. Of course, someone always had to be at the top of the food chain too.

They'd created this equilibrium out of the ashes of the

plague years, and it was his kingdom in which to rule. Nothing was going to end that, as far as he was concerned.

Damien began to flick through the papers on his desk. Even in Utopia paperwork had to be done. He scanned the names and one in particular caught his eye: Lucy Slater.

Isn't that the daughter of Talya Slater? he thought, placing the paper back on his work area and keying the name into his terminal to check her files.

Name: Slater, Lucy

Parents: Slater, Tom and Slater, Talya

He was right, names didn't usually jump out at him like that, but that Slater woman was such a pain in the neck, she was beginning to feel like an insomniac mosquito. She had that uncanny ability to charm large groups of people. She'd been used as a legal expert on one of the debates shown on the screens and somehow, bit by bit, she'd gained a massive following among both rich and poor in The City. They loved her fire and passion. She was dangerous, he knew. Most people he could just remove if they became a nuisance, but Talya had supporters. If she disappeared without explanation, that might cause trouble for him.

So what was Slater's daughter up to if she'd caught the attention of the Centuria? Damien picked up the file again and carried on reading. This might be just the chance he'd been waiting for.

Inside The Climbs

However many times Joe sprinted up the fifty-two flights of stairs, he could never do it in less than eleven minutes. When he was younger it was one of the big challenges of his tower, trying to achieve fifty floors in nine minutes. The problem was you never climbed them empty-handed, it was one of the unwritten rules of The Climbs.

Within every dilapidated tower block was a community of people: babies, seniors, those with disabilities. There was no welfare here beyond basic subsistence, not in The Climbs. You lived or died, the world wasn't particularly worried about it. They alone took care of each other, with the able-bodied residents bringing water and food for those who couldn't make it up or down the stairs.

You had to carry if you could. That was how people survived, and that's why Joe was always weighed down when he went up or down the stairs. He was fit, young and healthy, and he made enough currency on the black market to feed his mum, his brother and himself, so he felt it his duty to ferry more than he should have. Many were incarcerated in those concrete tombs, fated never to leave until they were carried out dead.

People like Joe and his friends were in high demand. They'd learned tech skills that enabled people to patch up what they could afford to buy if they were lucky enough to have employment.

He reached floor fifty, stepped off the staircase and moved towards Zach Fuller's door. As he went to knock, the door crashed to the ground. It had been barely hanging on to its hinges for months; the door had finally given up the battle and fallen off with a simple strike.

'That you, Joe?' came a voice from inside.

Joe heard the tap of Zach's makeshift crutches as they struck the concrete floor. He'd lost a leg in a factory accident three years ago, and the stairs were no longer a safe option for him.

'Damn, Zach, that door's had it. Are you going to be okay in here on your own?'

'Don't you worry, Joe, I've still got the knife you brought me, and I keep it with me all the time.'

Joe wondered how Zach could fight off any intruders when he needed two crutches just to stand up, but he also knew how determined this man was. He'd survived an amputation without anaesthetic – a privilege denied to most people living in The Climbs, especially those who'd just lost their job after an industrial accident.

Joe placed the provisions and water on Zach's battered table, dropping some bread on the floor as he did so. A large rat emerged from under the cupboard and made a dash at the ready-made meal. Joe jumped as he realized what was moving across the room in his direction. In an instant, Zach drew the knife from his belt and threw it with lethal accuracy, stopping the creature dead in its tracks. Joe figured that Zach could take care of himself after all.

'Hope you don't mind if I leave you to clear up?'

Zach laughed. 'No worries son, I know you hate the things, I've been after that one for weeks now.' Joe smiled at Zach, picked up the remainder of the provisions for his family and headed out towards the doorless entrance.

'See you tomorrow Zach!' called Joe as he departed. 'You want me to prop the door up before I go?'

'Leave it,' came the reply. 'Anybody intends to steal what's mine, they've got fifty levels to climb before they do. I reckon they'll be so tired out when they get here, I'll just be able to blow them over if they try it.'

Joe smiled to himself and started making his way up the final two flights. He hoped that he'd be as resilient as his neighbour if he were ever thrown on his own resources like that. He didn't know it then, as he walked into his home to be welcomed by his mum and brother, but he'd be needing some courage like that in the days that followed.

The Old World

Talya reached Harry's floor, exhausted by the climb. Her daughter Lucy had boasted that she could manage Joe's fifty-two flights in less than twelve minutes – and she didn't doubt it – but for her, progress was much slower. Still, she knew it would be worth it; she'd never spent time with Harry that had been wasted; she was a mine of useful information.

Not many books had survived the plague years, and those that did exist had to be held in a secure area of the Fortrillium building by decree of the Law Lords. This was for archiving purposes apparently, but Talya knew that it was more about suppressing the truth and creating a new timeline. A more convenient version of their history. Life according to Damien Hunter probably.

She despised the man, and she knew how much he hated her too. She understood that she was a threat to him, but there was nothing he could do about it – yet. Her power and influence within both city communities was too far-reaching. If the screens were ever switched off, that might change quickly, but Hunter relied on these to sedate and misinform the people.

Talya caught her breath at the top of the staircase and mopped her forehead with a handkerchief. She felt ridiculous as she did it – she'd passed babies who were barely clothed as she made her way up the stairs, how dare she even pay any attention to her own discomfort?

Talya knocked at the door. She knew to give it several hard bangs, as Harry was losing her hearing.

'Come in, Talya!' came a bright voice. Harry was incredible, 103 and still sounding like she was only sixty.

Talya gave the old lady a hug. Harry welcomed her

visits – most people dared not even talk about the pre-plague years. For her, it was the world that she'd been born into, and she wanted to remember, even if there did end up being consequences for her.

Talya put her hand into her bag and felt around, eventually drawing out what had been secreted in the lining.

'I got you these.' She handed the packets to Harry. 'I don't know how long until I'll be able to get my hands on more.'

Harry thanked her. The drugs that Talya had smuggled in would help to reduce the pain of her arthritis.

'Damn getting old!' she cursed to herself. Her mind was still sharp and agile, if only her body could keep up.

Talya prepared some food for her friend, making a hot drink on the gas stove that Lucy and Joe had managed to procure on her behalf. They sat down by Harry's window and gazed out over the city.

'What lies beyond the boundary, Harry?' asked Talya. 'Is there anything left there now?'

There was a glint in Harry's eyes. It was forbidden to say what she was about to say, but who cared? What could they do to a 103-year-old lady now?

'That depends on who you ask, Talya – Damien Hunter or me.'

Incarcerated

Clay Hillman had had one week to get used to life in The Soak. There were rumours about this place, where it was and what it was like. Nobody ever got out of here anyway. Once you'd been sent to The Soak your time was up, there was no release.

They were right about the soak bit. It was so wet in his

cell that there was a constant dripping from the river bed above.

They were in a vast circular underground dungeon. Hundreds of cages surrounded the walls, and each enclosure housed ten detainees – he reckoned there were several thousand people incarcerated there.

Every cage was accessible via a narrow walkway. There were only four ladders down to exit or enter the containers, and these were placed at quarter points. The steps were retracted unless someone new was coming in or leaving. Most of the time people only came in. The only time anybody got out was when they'd chosen to seek justice in The Grid.

The cells were mixed gender – women, children, youngsters, the elderly, they all suffered in the same cages. The sanitation was perfunctory, only open toilets with no showers, and food and water were delivered via automated hatches built into the concrete walls at the rear of every cell.

You got to eat if you were strong enough to fight for what came through the upper hatch. If you weren't assertive enough, you died, and then you left through the small trap that was placed at the front of each cage before you started to decompose and stink the place out. If anybody noticed, that is.

Clay sat in the corner of his prison, still not used to the stench given off by his nine companions, all of whom had been there much longer than himself. He surveyed the vast central watchtower from which they were monitored twenty-four hours a day, large rapid-fire guns aimed at them continually in case of any unrest.

He was in a cell with four females and five other men. The women were scared for their lives, terrified by one of the men in particular who had been jailed for violence.

Clay knew that sooner or later he'd have to confront the man and take the consequences. That's if they couldn't all team up and sort him out between them.

They had been too intimidated. Two of the men were nearly dead, and the other two didn't seem as if they were capable of putting up a defence. It would probably end up with Clay intervening, but if he made too much fuss about it the shots would begin.

He'd seen it already on his second day when a fight broke out in one of the cages overhead. Without warning the guns began to fire from the tower – all of the inhabitants of that cell were gunned down, no questions asked about the cause or the instigator of the trouble. The deaths were followed by a flush of water from above. This usually sufficed for a shower in The Soak. As the bloody water from the upper cages turned clear, Clay had realized that an arm had washed its way through the grilles and come to rest at his side. By the time he'd woken up from a restless sleep, the rats had taken it, there was just bone left on the floor.

Whatever Clay did to sort out the maniac, it would have to be done quickly and quietly. After only a week in The Soak he was beginning to think that it might be worth taking his chances in The Grid.

CHAPTER THREE

The President

Damien sat in the uncomfortable wooden chair that had been put out for him in the President's office. He was sure that nobody else had to endure the discomfort of that godforsaken, battered old thing. It was a torture that President Josh Delman reserved just for him. It was no secret that there was no love lost between Damien and Delman, but they were forced by necessity to work together. Fortrillium wouldn't exist without there being a form of governance within The City. They'd just be a bunch of bully boys without their legal remit – and the government couldn't survive and maintain the peace without Fortrillium. It was a stalemate, but Josh Delman was the senior of the two, and he wasted no time reminding Damien of that fact at every opportunity. In every meeting, Damien would be left on his own in that threadbare chair facing the President's massive polished wooden desk and his comfortable leather seat. He would ponder if there might be a time in the future that he might get to sit in Delman's place and have overall control of The City.

Certainly Fortrillium was powerful enough, and it afforded Damien the cover he needed to achieve outcomes that were advantageous to his career and standing. If a particular high-ranking official were to find themselves condemned to The Soak as a result of charges of corruption arising from Centuria 'evidence', who was to argue? If the occasional political agitator 'disappeared' without trace, who would dare put up much fuss if they'd been forced to enter The Grid before they got a chance for justice? And if an official or two were to go missing and the only witness to have an unfortunate accident soon after, would anybody worry about that in the grand scheme of things? Damien thought not. In fact, he knew not.

For those on Silk Road, life in The City could be sweet. The people who held all the power, influence and money lived on the outer perimeter, and because their lives were so perfect they never needed to wonder what lay beyond that. Besides, Fortrillium Information, the public service division of the corporation, kept them fully updated about life outside the high city walls.

The plague was still out there, having left billions across the planet dead in its wake. Former cities were deserted and crumbling, and this, their city, was the only refuge. They were safe in this sanctuary, they had food, heat, water, shelter and comfort ... lots of it too, if you were fortunate enough to live in the outer perimeter.

Those on the inside were effectively imprisoned by Segregation. This meant that although Silk Roaders could enter The Climbs, the reverse was not possible without a permit. And those permits were hard to come by, extending mainly to work-related duties.

Curfew was enforced between 20:00 until 06:00 every day, and this controlled the flow of people in a way that made resistance impossible. With the firm arm of Damien's Centuria controlling legal matters throughout The City, the best option remained to keep your head down and get on with your lot, whatever that was.

Even though Damien Hunter would have balked at any such crass suggestion, an outsider looking in might comment that this had every appearance of astute social engineering. The poor kept in their place, the rich made so comfortable that they had no need to complain; the fear of death beyond the city walls, and a powerful policing force threatened anybody who dared to challenge the status quo. Plus a legal system that was formidable and unbeatable: the Law Lords and The Grid. It meant, for all intents and purposes, that Fortrillium – or Damien – was the law.

That's why he was sitting in that unforgiving wooden chair at that moment. He wanted to petition the President about his recent tactical move to promote Talya Slater to the position of Law Lord. There were seven Law Lords in all, each one a respected member of the Silk Road community. 'Respected' generally meant 'chosen by Damien Hunter'.

Damien had made an error of judgement by removing a Law Lord unceremoniously from the panel. What that entailed in reality was that this particular Law Lord had been found dead, thrown from the top of one of the tower blocks in The Climbs, having been mysteriously trapped in there after curfew. Nobody knew why he was out after Segregation, what he was doing or who would want him flung from the top of a high-rise. Neither could the Centuria find any witnesses or evidence, after what seemed to some to be a brief, even cursory, investigation. That left Damien with the problem of finding a replacement. Surprisingly enough he had just the person in mind, an influential businessman from Silk Road, who ardently supported the good work of Fortrillium, particularly under Damien's leadership.

President Josh Delman had other ideas. He was not driven by the same base desires as Damien Hunter, his priorities were more political than self-serving, though, of course, it all boiled down to the same thing in the end. Josh Delman had a leadership to sustain. His position was preserved through a combination of public charm and background control, whereas Damien seldom felt the need to exhibit any charm at all.

That's what this meeting was about. Delman was forcing his choice of replacement Law Lord. Hunter was resisting. This particular Law Lord could cause all sorts of trouble for him. Delman's acute political sense told him that a well-placed Law Lord would help to maintain harmony within The City. Hunter's survival instincts knew that if this particular Law Lord made it to the panel, things could become difficult for him.

Most Law Lords could be offered sweeteners to lean the way that Damien wanted them to. If the sweeteners didn't work, then a threat often did the job. And if threats didn't work? Well, being thrown off the top of a tower block usually resolved that little matter. That was what had forced Damien into the President's office for this particular meeting. He was not at all happy with Delman's choice, and he'd come to protest against it in no uncertain terms.

As President Josh Delman finally entered his office, a full ten minutes after the meeting was supposed to have begun, Damien knew that he was in for a tough time. It would be difficult convincing him not to assign the popular Talya Slater to the panel of Law Lords. But if the President insisted on forcing through the appointment, he had an excellent counter-play up his sleeve which would stop Slater dead in her tracks.

Taken

It always surprised Joe how much he could remember about that day. He must have been only twelve years old at the time, his brother nine, but every detail of it was still so clear that it might have just happened hours ago.

He'd been aware that things were tense at home. They lived on Silk Road in those days, and he was used to his parents talking about things of which he had little understanding. It hadn't particularly bothered him at the time – there was just an awareness that something was going on, and it probably wasn't good.

Matt Parsons had been on the senior management staff at Fortrillium, under Damien Hunter. The Parsons family were close friends with the Slaters. That's why Lucy and Joe were such firm allies, they'd known each other for years. At first they'd played together as kids, latterly they'd been planning and colluding together, as their adult selves realized at long last what had been going on at that time. Tom Slater – Lucy's dad – had worked with Matt at Fortrillium, and that's how the families had got to know each other. Joe could also recall earnest and hushed conversations between Matt and Tom. He'd just assumed it was 'adult stuff', before the Centuria arrived at their house.

It was late in the evening, after Segregation, and Joe and his family were watching the screen and catching up with the latest news from The City. Having a screen in the house was just one of the luxuries of Silk Road. If you wanted to watch a screen in The Climbs, you usually had to stand outside or look out of your window. Only a handful of people there had personal access, usually via the black market or some form of subterfuge. You didn't boast about it, that would encourage a call from the Centuria, wondering how you'd managed to procure such expensive equipment and a power supply to make it work.

There was no knock on the door, not even any conversation. Four Centuria burst into the house, electro-cuffed Matt and started to march him out at gunpoint. The only humanity shown was when Matt protested that he should be able to say goodbye to his family. It cost him a bloody blow to his head from a gun butt, but he got his request. A quick hug for Jena, Dillon and Joe and he was away. That was the last they saw of him, he never came back after that. You'd have to be pretty quick to have spotted it, but he lingered just a little longer with Joe, slipping something small into his pocket before he was forced away by the Centuria. Joe was about to ask what it was that he'd been given. Even at that young age, he was wise enough to stay quiet – something in him sensed that his father had just handed over an item of critical importance.

Matt was marched out of the house and driven away in a black, windowless truck under armed guard. The front door was open, and there was silence in the house, they were stunned by what had happened.

Within moments, more vehicles drew up outside. Heavy boots were heard marching up to the door: more Centuria, probably different people, but they all had the same appearance in their black, menacing uniforms. Jena, Dillon and Joe were escorted out of their house, thrown into a large, cold truck that had been parked outside the house, and driven into The Climbs. There were to be no courtesies or explanations about this. The remaining family members were dumped in the centre of The Climbs in the darkness of the night and left there to fend for themselves. Joe could remember every detail. He recalled sitting with his sobbing mother, turning the device that his father had given him over and over in his hand. He realized that he was going to have to take charge of the family.

Jena was never the same after that night. It broke her. Although she had two young boys to protect and support, it was Joe who rose to the challenge and who became the new provider for the family. They lived on the streets for two nights, going without food and drinking water from the puddles that had formed on the broken pavements.

Soon a man called Zach came along, took pity on them and offered to help. There was an empty apartment two flights up from him. The previous user had jumped after finding out that he'd got a terminal illness. There were few drugs in The Climbs; it was easier and quicker to jump if you got seriously ill, and everybody knew that.

The remaining members of the Parsons family moved into Magnum Block, and that was their new home. Among the rats, filth and squalor. A decaying tower block, seventy-five storeys high and named after some powerful business magnate from before the plague.

Joe thought he'd seen his dad's face on the screen outside their block, but Zach had hurried him away, telling him not to bother with such trivial rubbish. Zach had become quite forceful. Joe thought he'd heard mention of The Grid in the news commentary, but he'd been pulled away by then, he couldn't hear the rest. That was when Zach had both his legs. It's why Joe thought nothing of bringing him food every day, Zach had once done the same for them. It's how people survived in The Climbs.

It was a bleak time, and one which Joe could recall with

clarity. They never knew what became of Matt immediately after his arrest, but Joe had been able to discover later that he had been sent to The Grid. Jena was too broken to care, she just existed most days. If Joe hadn't stepped up, they'd all have died out there on the streets.

In spite of all that had happened, it might have been worse. At precisely the same time that the Centuria broke down the door of Joe's house, the Slaters had received a late-night knock at their door. Tom Slater had disappeared without a trace. His WristCom had stopped transmitting data. Strangely, there were no witnesses and no body.

Preparation

Max Penner began the activation sequence for the cleaner bots. There were twenty in all, all about half his height, made out of metal and built for heavy industrial use. They used a combination of cleaners, spinners, cutters and grinders – Max didn't like to think about it too much.

It was his job to release the bots into The Grid. No human was permitted to step into the arena unless it was to seek justice. The bots entered a long dark tunnel via his control area, but there were five more iron doors to go through before they even accessed The Grid. There was no chance of Max ever getting a view of what was in there. There were no cameras switched on until the environment had been rendered for Justice Seeking.

Fortrillium only let you see what they wanted you to see. They saved that for the screens, and to Max's knowledge nobody at his level had ever got to see in there. Besides, it might have sounded like a prime job, being at the heart of the legal system, but all he did was to program the bots for cleaning and maintenance.

They'd make their long journey up the tunnels, clean up after the trial, and then return to the warehouse area for Max to deal with the waste. The bots left him empty and returned to him full. He didn't like to dwell too much on what the bots contained. They took care of the cutting and grinding that was required for disposal, and then they would auto-connect to the pipelines and eject their contents.

Max only had to get involved every once in a while, but like everything mechanical, sometimes the bots would get a jam. When those things stuck, you needed to get your overalls on and make sure your stomach was firmly in place. In the past Max had removed the lower part of an arm, a left foot and a crushed skull from blocked pipes. They smelled terrible too – many of the bodies had begun decomposing, but there was no retrieval of bodies until after the trial was over.

The skull was the latest blockage that he'd had to clear, and it had taken some time to get the bot going again. Usually he could shut off his feelings from the ugliness of his work. His was a privileged role. He'd been allocated a small and plainly furnished house on Silk Road when he'd been given the job – it was a blessed relief after a lifetime being brought up in The Climbs. On a regular day, he'd just get on with it, satisfying himself that was how things were, it was not up to him to challenge The City's system of justice. That day was different, though, it had spooked him.

Normally he could detach himself from what was going on inside The Grid. But the skull had changed things. It had just been stuck there in the wide circular mouth of the bot's pipework. He'd taken an hour to get it out and remove the blockage. And all through that time he'd been face-to-face with the crushed bones of the man called Jay, who he'd watched on his home screen perishing in The Grid only hours before.

Memory

Talya knew that if Josh Delman's campaign played out she'd never be able to get back into The Climbs unobserved. Once she was a Law Lord – if that's what happened – she'd have to stay well away, she'd be more scrutinized than she'd ever been before in her life.

Delman had first approached her a couple of days previously. It seemed remarkable after the disappearance of Tom six years before that her climb to such heights should have been so meteoric. Whereas Jena had caved in at the time, it had made Talya stronger. It was just her and Lucy. They'd avoided being sent to The Climbs, unlike the Parsons family. Tom had to have been on to something at Fortrillium, there must have been a reason he and Matt were so hastily disposed of. There was no proof that Tom had been murdered, of course – all the theories of the Centuria pointed towards a motiveless crime. He must have been in The Climbs for some purpose – he never went there usually. The only clue was that Tom's WristCom was missing, the last signal received from it had originated in The Climbs.

Talya was not stupid, she was a survivor. She knew then that it was not the time to challenge. She had to grieve for the loss of her husband, regroup with Lucy – and survive. They had to be grateful for the small mercies that they'd been given, tiny scraps in which to find some solace. She hoped that Tom had died quickly, without fear, if that's how he'd met his end.

Matt's death had been prolonged. He'd sought justice in

The Grid, and lost. He'd survived in there over two weeks. The screen audiences were massive, and Matt had been an inspirational leader guiding his fellow Justice Seekers to survival for over fourteen days. Nobody had ever seen such an incredible trial in the history of The Grid, and Matt had almost become a hero.

Just as it seemed as if this team of Justice Seekers might make it out alive, things took a sudden turn. The Centuria uncovered evidence that Matt had been involved in a funding scandal, siphoning off and selling valuable aid that was destined to help the needy in The Climbs. On top of that, his bedraggled team of fellow Justice Seekers had additional information leaked about their pasts. It seemed there were child-killers, thieves who took food from the elderly, and evil predators among them. Public opinion turned, the situation within The Grid itself pivoted without warning – as if a new person were in control – and the survivors perished, one by one. Each death was greeted by the cheers of the misinformed crowds who'd bought wholesale the spurious information disseminated by Fortrillium Information. Originating from the desk of Damien Hunter.

Talya had hung on until the end to watch Matt's final moments. Somebody needed to know for Jena. Someone had to bear witness for her. Talya knew that Jena wasn't watching. She'd asked Zach to protect the boys from the trial, but one day Joe and Dillon would be men, they'd want to know what happened to their father. It was the least that she could do for them, to be able to tell them how bravely their father had fought before he died.

She'd forced herself to watch the screen at the end, but fortunately she was spared Matt's final moments, as were the rest of the population in The City. A technical problem shut off all the screens in The City in the last minutes of

Matt's trial. It was certain that he couldn't escape anyway. It was clear that there was no way out for him. In those final, terrible moments, Matt had shouted something. It sounded like 'You head for the core, Joe …' but it was meaningless out of context. The sound feed went down, then the picture and it was over. Matt was dead, the same as Tom. Whatever they'd been talking about at work, whatever plot they'd been making, it had gone to the grave with them.

Talya realized a couple of years afterwards that Tom and Matt had probably given them a precious gift by not sharing the information with their wives. If all the parents had been taken away, what would have happened to the children? Talya shuddered, she couldn't bear the thought of Lucy being left to perish in The Climbs. She'd had to be tough – she needed to survive for both of them. Lucy was becoming an adult, and she was strong in her own way. Talya could focus on getting her revenge. It had taken every bit of courage, cunning, planning and strategy that she could muster.

Her pro bono work in The Climbs had made her hugely popular among its residents. Her legal activities on behalf of the wealthy of Silk Road had given her access to some of the most influential people in The City. She'd worked her contacts, rich and poor, and her appearances on the screens had boosted her fame and popularity. The citizens loved her passion and fire. She was in that unique position of being liked by both sides. It was this that President Josh Delman had noticed and was the reason for him nurturing her as an ally. She was a perfect and timely addition to the unpopular panel of Law Lords, she alone would help Delman to revive his profile and image.

Damien Hunter had recognized her as a danger many years ago, but he felt unable to move with Delman breathing down his neck. She had the flimsy protection of the President. There were to be no mysterious accidents for Talya Slater. Damien had seriously considered for a while the possibility of staging her public murder in The Climbs, by some drugged-up resident. Unusually for him, he'd called off the assassination at the last moment, thinking better of it and deciding to wait for a more suitable opportunity to strike.

Talya tuned back into Harry's voice. She was remarkable for 103 years old, but she did tend to wander a little. Talya had to focus – if this was the last time she'd be able to make a visit, she needed to pump Harry for as much knowledge as she could. Harry loved to talk about the days before the plague, the twins, her brother and parents. She couldn't help herself getting distracted by who did what and when, rather than giving Talya the valuable information that she craved.

What lay beyond the city walls, what was out there? Harry was hazy on the details.

It was a long time ago. She wished her friends were still alive so that she could clarify the facts; she was so old that she had to make a real effort to separate what was genuine from what was imagination.

Indeed, the plague had come quickly. It had killed millions, probably billions. There had been riots, civil unrest, violence and destruction. Everybody carried the disease; some managed to survive it, though.

She couldn't recall where The City was based. She thought either the USA or the UK, but these terms were meaningless to Talya, they only knew 'The City', it was all most of them had ever known. She understood that Fortrillium was telling lies about what happened in the past, but so many years of their untruths and she'd forgotten what was real and what was not. Harry had fallen ill with the plague, she recalled being in an aircraft, but couldn't remember which country she'd started in and which country she'd ended up in. Talya had never seen an aircraft, she found it hard to imagine what one was.

There was a swift recovery for Harry. She was lucky, she'd developed immunity. Her parents knew influential people, and they took her to a secret place – underground, if she remembered correctly. But she was only a child then, seeing things through a child's eyes, it was so long ago, and her memories were hazy. Talya couldn't delay it any longer, this was her last visit, it was almost Segregation, and she had to leave Harry and try and get her to recollect.

'Harry, who was it who survived The Grid ... who got out of there alive?'

A direct question, but it was unlikely that she'd get an immediate answer. But she was wrong. Harry ceased what she was saying and paused.

'Do you know what, Talya? I can remember at long last. It just came to me in a flash, I don't know why I ever forgot!'

She stopped herself again as if to check her memory files and make sure that what she was about to say was correct.

'It was the President, Talya. It was Josh Delman.'

CHAPTER FOUR

Sewers

'I wish there was a way of doing this without having to come down here!' said Joe.

The stench of the drains was unbearable. He was beginning to yearn for one of the others to do his work. When the time came though, it had to be him – the data card had genetic encryption. Mitchell and Wiz were excellent at the above-ground stuff. When it came to crouching in a sewer up to your knees in who knows what and braving the rats, it was, unfortunately, a job for Joe Parsons.

Lucy was there, though. She always was and always had been since his dad had been taken away. Lucy who got to shower every day, who had managed to hang on in the family home after her father had died and who lived a life of luxury on the other side of the wall. She could come to him, but he couldn't cross to her side. She was the same that she'd always been, she smuggled in whatever contraband that she could, but she couldn't be seen to break the rules. Everybody knew where that ended up.

Still, she was content to crouch in a foul sewer with him and that said a lot. Lucy was supporting the mass of wires that they'd managed to access through the roof of the pipeline. They'd made progress last time they were down there – they knew that data was not only flowing through Fortrillium, but there was also a source outside it. Another location? A government agency perhaps? Or might it have come from beyond The City's walls?

This was Mitchell's skill, figuring out the Fortrillium network layout and – most importantly – where they could breach it. Mitchell was from Silk Road too. His mum was involved in infrastructure developments, and it wasn't difficult to get the information if you knew what you were looking for. Using this mess of wires and some tech assembled from components that Lucy had smuggled in, they'd created an interface from which they could hack into Fortrillium. It was Matt's files that they were after though – if they still existed on the server. That was where Lucy came in. She was in charge of network forensics.

Life was sweet if you lived on Silk Road. You got taught via screens and started training for work from fourteen years old. It was different in The Climbs. There was no education, only manual employment – or death. Joe survived by his wits. He didn't take a job, but he'd spent enough time on Silk Road to have the basics that he needed, the rest he'd taught himself.

Zach's books had helped too. Joe hadn't told anybody about that, not even Lucy. If he were ever found out, Zach was a dead man. He'd never survive incarceration with his disabilities, and he'd die in The Grid in an instant.

Lucy had been learning about network forensics for three years. She was good – excellent – and through her mum she'd gained entry-level access to one of the few tech companies that existed in The City. Like Joe, Lucy was a survivor, she was quite capable of teaching herself. So while they kept her occupied with mostly menial and meaningless tasks, she was way ahead of them, learning so fast that she could outpace the majority of the employees at the company.

The plan was for Mitchell to find the way into Fortrillium, for Wiz to get them connected, and for Joe to activate whatever it was that his dad had given him before the Centuria took him. Lucy was to get the residual data, which must have been deleted or hidden in the aftermath of Matt's demise. If they got lucky, Lucy might also find some of her own dad's files. That was unlikely. Unique DNA password protection at Fortrillium was commonplace, it was one of the few technologies that had survived and flourished after the plague. It was as if somebody had something that they were keen to hide, there would be no way into Tom's files without some sort of assistance, like Joe had been given.

Matt had handed Joe the electronic data card, but it was domestic, it could only be opened by someone with the same genetics – any family member. Joe and his gang had got into the gadget quite quickly a few years previously, but the data was encrypted, Fortrillium had locked it. They needed to run the apparatus via Fortrillium's network – they had to hack the system.

They'd spent several nights down the sewers, trying to stitch everything together to make it work. They'd fumbled around in the stinking darkness, achieving what they could, and then trying to patch up the problems above ground, using whatever resources Lucy could smuggle in. All of this without arousing any suspicion. Damn, it was hard. But they sensed that they were almost there. If they could just access the network, they were sure that they'd finally be able to unveil some of Fortrillium's darkest secrets. Joe and Lucy would eventually find out what had happened to their fathers, they would know the truth at last, even though they had no idea what they would do with it.

Without warning, there was a cry of panic from Wiz at the head of the sewer. Mitchell wasn't with them that night, he'd had to stay on the Silk Road side, and that meant Wiz had got distracted. Lucy jumped. Joe glanced along the long pipe-way towards the darkness. They'd got carried away, they'd lost track of time. It was two minutes until Segregation – there was insufficient time to make it past the security gate. Lucy was trapped in The Climbs for the night. It was impossible to make it to the end of the sewer pipe and get to the checkpoint in time. Any excuses would fall on deaf ears. If she got caught by the Centuria, there would be no forgiveness for Lucy Slater.

Gridder

There were wild cheers as Hannah slammed her opponent to the ground, did a back flip that involved an impossibly high leap, then landed on her combatant's chest. With a sharp kick, he was out cold, yet here was Hannah, a fraction of his height and weight.

It was the annual Gridder contest, a high profile gaming event on Silk Road in which the best gamers in The City competed for the chance to become that year's champion. For the winner, it meant fame, good fortune and popularity.

The Gridder Games were based on real-life scenarios in The Grid, though, in this case, nobody died. The opponent Hannah had floored was just a pixel image on an enormous screen that was being watched by a seated crowd of over five hundred people.

It was her dexterity and speed, rather than her strength, which had caused her to win. Hannah had won that year's championship. She'd been practising for months from the comfort of her well-equipped home on Silk Road, a privilege denied to the residents of The Climbs.

After the celebrations had died down, Hannah decided to take the long way home. She'd been cooped up in front of screens all day, and she wanted to focus her eyes on something different. As she left the gaming complex, she felt an intense sensation of being followed, but in spite of looking back several times, she could see no evidence to support that theory. The feeling persisted, and she began to think better of having strayed into one of the most remote areas of Silk Road.

Hannah walked out of the park area, onto the walkway, and as she did so – apparently from nowhere – three large black cars drew up at her side. Centuria emerged from the front and back vehicles; one of them opened the passenger door of the middle car and Damien Hunter stepped out. Hannah knew who he was immediately, his face was all over the screens, and Fortrillium pretty well ran The City.

'Hannah James,' he began. 'I'm Damien Hunter, congratulations on your win today, that was an impressive performance!'

Hannah wasn't sure what tack to take. Usually a visit from so many Centuria meant bad news. This seemed to be a social call, their stance was respectful rather than threatening. They didn't appear to want to throw her into the boot of one of those vehicles. Hannah opted for the friendly approach.

'Thanks a lot, Mr Hunter, pleased to meet you,' she replied. 'I know you're a big fan of the Gridder Games.'

'I certainly am, that's why I was so keen to get to know you. I watch the results of the tournament carefully.'

Hannah wondered what was coming next, this was leading to something, and she could see him manoeuvring the conversation towards the point of his visit.

'Hannah, I need you to sign this document. What I'm about to discuss with you is covered by a government secrecy clause. It's imperative that you don't mention this little chat to anybody.'

Hannah was intrigued and also wary, Damien Hunter tended not to drop in on social calls. Could she say 'no'? She suspected that wasn't an option. One of the Centuria handed her an e-Doc device and she flicked through the legal text.

'I know it seems convoluted,' said Damien, 'but all it says is that our conversation is between us only and must remain private.'

Hannah scanned the paperwork swiftly. Damien was right, it used a lot of complicated language to say just that. However, he missed out the bit that was tucked away at the bottom of the page.

'This document is bound by Government Secrecy Clause 3.f.v4.5 LL.'

The sting was contained in the letters 'LL' which meant that this particular breach of the law would be referred to the Law Lords, which in turn entailed incarceration. Hannah wasn't sure what to do, but she was fascinated to know what this was about. It seemed simple enough. She'd signed the Citizen Contract when she was fourteen years old, just like every other city dweller had. The 'LL' was a veiled threat, but like any laws, play by the rules and it was never any bother.

Hannah decided to sign. This clause only related to

their conversation, it would be easy enough to keep that quiet, she wasn't signing her life away, not yet at least. She pressed her thumb on the signature panel; the sensor did not detect sufficient sweat, so a small pinprick of blood was taken to determine and confirm identity. With that over, the e-Doc device was handed back to the Centuria and placed in a secure case that was then locked.

Hannah wasn't sure if she could have resisted these overtures even if she'd tried. She desperately wanted to know why someone like Damien Hunter had stopped her in the street on such intriguing business. She'd heard the rumours just like everybody else, but she supposed that the reason they'd remained only whispers was because all the others had had to sign a document just as she had. It had been her motivation for pushing hard to win the Gridder Games too – apart from the prestige – she wondered if the hearsay was true.

They'd all seen The Justice Trials on the screens. All residents of The City grew up with them, but those who were a little more perceptive speculated about who was behind The Grid and how those justice challenges were created. A few had noticed in recent times that things seemed to change at the end. Many on trial had nearly made it to the Justice Walk, but in the last moments it appeared that no person was ever supposed to make it beyond The Grid. It was as if a final executioner was lying in wait to rob them of life, even though they might have survived many days to get as far as they had.

The suspicion in The City was – and nobody dared speak this theory in open conversation – that champion Gridders were secretly approached by Fortrillium to help to create The Justice Trials. This was why Hannah could not resist signing the paperwork. She knew for sure that she was speaking to a monster, but by completing that document she would move closer to the truth. It appeared that the rumours were correct, it was not more than three hours since she'd won the contest and already here was Damien Hunter courting her directly.

Hannah understood exactly what she was getting herself into – what they were all getting themselves into. At least she wasn't knee-deep in the sewers, though, like Wiz, Lucy and Joe. Thanks to her gaming abilities, she'd been the obvious choice for this particular role, the particulars of which she had every intention of sharing with her group of friends.

Challenge

Clay watched as the predator in the cage picked the man up by his neck, lifting him away from the floor, slowly choking him and looking directly into his eyes as he did so. It had been like this all week, but as the most recent addition to the cell he hadn't started to intimidate Clay yet. Still too much strength in him no doubt. A few weeks on the hopelessly inadequate rations in The Soak and Clay would begin to weaken too.

There was no justice in this legal system, as Clay had learned already. The strongest in the cell got most of the food, the remainder got what was left after he'd finished. As the rest got weaker, he'd threaten them and make their lives a misery, eventually killing them.

They'd lost two of the men and one of the women in the past three days. Clay had tried to intervene, but the madman was too strong, he was just brushed aside and thrown into the corner. He was lucky they had not been spotted by the guards, he'd expected them to open fire at any moment. It would be Clay's turn soon. He would prob-ably be choked in the night just like one of the other men. There was no attempt to segregate inmates based on the levels of their crimes, and they'd found themselves caged in with a psychotic murderer. Talk about drawing the short straw.

Clay knew that he'd have to act – he had done so from the minute he'd clocked what this man was capable of. It was kill or be killed, either way there was unlikely to be a happy ending in all of this.

He'd been in The Soak for long enough to figure out the routine, even if it was so darn difficult to keep track of the time in there. It was underground, so there was no natural daylight. The patterns of the day were dictated by food, staff changeovers and the level of dripping from the river bed above them. At certain times of day, the seepage would increase; although Clay didn't know it, this was due to tidal ebbs and flows on the surface overhead.

Clay had never seen the sea, neither had anybody else in The City, except for a few people who were from the first generation, but not many of those were still alive. Clay reck-oned that the psychopath had timed his attack just right. They should be flushing out the cages soon. That meant an almighty gush of water would come cascading through the cells, starting at the top and working its way to the bottom, bringing with it all the filth and dirt from the inmates. It was as close as things got to hygiene in The Soak, but it seemed fairly effective in keeping disease out – possibly something was added to the water.

If that man could keep breathing until the flush came, Clay thought, he might be able to sort out the problem they had in their cell. The big, violent and brutal one.

He was right. He heard the discharge of the water from

above. They were five cages down as far as he could tell, and the water would fall fast and hard on them. The minute the release came, most inmates threw themselves to the floor and let it wash over them. You only tried fighting it once – the water came through the bars with such a force that it thrust the inmates to the ground anyway.

You never knew what was coming down with it either. Your best bet was to throw yourself on the floor, belly down, and protect the back of your head with clasped hands. All sorts worked their way down through the cages: rats, body parts, human waste, and the occasional weapon or dangerous object. If one of those hit you on the head, you could be a goner.

So when the flush began, Clay threw himself to the ground, by the feet of the monster who ignored the water and continued with his violent strangulation.

Clay waited for the water to make its way down, counting the cries as it smashed against the inhabitants of the cells higher up. One ... two ... three ... four ... Clay's cage next. Clay stood up before the water hit and ran with every bit of energy that he could summon towards the thighs of the killer. The thug was completely taken aback by this, tackled out of nowhere, and he dropped his victim as he fell heavily to the floor.

Clay heard the water strike the bars above him. He rushed at the assailant, wrenching his head upwards so that it would meet the powerful cascade of water as it made its way down from the upper cells. The water came thundering through the cell. He could hear the cries of his cell-mates as it stung their bodies, but Clay held the psycho's head directly towards the flow, forcing his jaw open. He hadn't been expecting the attack. He'd tried to inhale as his massive frame went crashing to the floor, and when the water came it washed into his open mouth as he struggled to draw in air.

As he drew breath, he took water into his lungs. Immediately his body reacted to repel the water. Clay felt him panic as air was denied, but the force was too overpowering. He gulped in more water, and there was a spasm as it washed into his stomach. Clay held him there in the path of the water until he went limp, and the water had passed through.

When the water had subsided, Clay broke his neck just to make sure, an action concealed by the other inmates who were standing once again now the coast was clear. The monster was dead, the cage was safe. He'd avoided the guns too – if the guards had seen them fighting, it would all have been over.

The killer had worked silently. His victims were no match for him, and so his kills were silent. If Clay had tackled him in open combat, it would have been loud, violent and nasty. This was the only way to finish it. The rats and the decomposition would take care of the rest, but at least they were safe for the time being.

The killer was no more. Only, to survive Clay himself had had to turn assassin. This was going to be life in The Soak. Clay was beginning to understand why taking his chances in The Grid might seem like a good idea.

Summons

Talya was staring into the eyes of the man who, only two hours earlier, she'd learned was the only survivor that anybody could remember ever making it out of The Grid alive. Harry had told her as much. She'd been sure of her facts on that one, it was a timely moment of clarity.

President Delman was old, that was for sure, possibly eighty years, perhaps a little younger. He was certainly still healthy and robust, sharp-minded and very much in charge, there was no doubt about that. But he'd been President for so long, there was no wonder that people like Harry could barely remember. It was just one of those things that you accepted. Josh Delman had always been President for as long as most people could recall.

The summons had come unexpectedly. She'd had to make her excuses and leave Harry at some speed. Delman required his seventh Law Lord, and he was set on Talya. He needed her sworn in as soon as possible. For Talya, that meant immediately.

The President had sent a car for her. She'd covered her tracks by claiming to be engaged in pro bono activities in The Climbs, making an excuse for being there rather than at work on Silk Road. She reckoned she'd got close to beating Lucy's record running back down the stairs of the tower block. She'd never run so fast in her life. She'd arranged to meet up with the car somewhere more general in The Climbs, she didn't want them getting any ideas about where she'd been at the particular moment they'd messaged her. Damn WristComs, they meant you could never truly get away.

The car drew up just as she arrived at the meeting place. She did her best to conceal her breathlessness, but the run down so many flights of stairs had got the better of her. She'd barely had time to say a proper goodbye to Harry before she went. She'd quickly explained how she would send Lucy with the drugs and provisions and that she wouldn't be able to visit anymore. Lucy spent enough time in The Climbs seeing Joe and the gang; she sometimes worried about her being there so much, but who was she to complain? They'd both felt a tremendous obligation to Joe and his family after they were evicted from Silk Road. They'd come within an inch of the same fate themselves, so the two of them were forever bound to life in The Climbs.

Talya held her gaze on President Delman as she repeated the words of the oath after him. She knew she was playing with fire, but how else could she get to the truth about Tom's assumed death? She had to move closer to the centre. That's where the answers were concealed.

Talya's senses told her that Damien Hunter was the enemy, not President Delman. With the latest information from Harry, the ageing man standing before her must have been athletic and active at one time if he ever made it through The Grid.

Why was he in there in the first place? she wondered.

The only way to cease being a Law Lord was through death – natural or otherwise – so this was no temporary arrangement. Wherever this was leading, Talya was committing to the whole journey. Once you'd experienced bereavement so close to you, you lost a certain amount of fear. If a loved one could make it through the last walk to death, you knew that you could too, there was comfort in that, it made the unknown a little less sinister.

Lucy was old enough to take care of herself. She hoped it would never come to that, but she owed it to Tom and Lucy – to the Parsons family too – to find out what happened on that terrible night.

'Congratulations Talya.' President Delman extended his hand. 'I'm delighted to welcome you as the seventh Law Lord. I know you'll be passionate about seeing that justice is done.'

'Thank you, President, it's an honour to join the panel, I'm extremely grateful for your sponsorship.'

President Delman ushered Talya to the side of the room. He wanted to speak privately.

'Between you and me, I want you to keep an eye on Hunter for me. Let me know if he makes any approaches to you, anything at all. We need to maintain a watch on that man.'

She hadn't been a Law Lord for more than five minutes and already Talya was being sucked in, she hadn't imagined that things would move quite so fast. Even more interesting was that Hunter had been delayed, he'd sent his apologies that he would be unable to make the ceremony in time. Important Fortrillium business to be attended to apparently, something that couldn't wait.

Talya knew the rest of the Law Lords already, through social contacts, though she would never have claimed to like any of them. This was what was making her give the President the benefit of the doubt, they all knew she'd be a thorn in everyone's side, he must have wanted her there to stir things up. The Chief Law Lord was Leianna Richwald, who happened to be friendly with Damien Hunter.

There were few super rich in Silk Road, five hundred or so, but Leianna was certainly one of them. In fact, every single one of the most affluent and influential people living in The City had a direct link, in one way or another, to Fortrillium. Except Talya, who'd rejected the trappings of her new role, preferring instead to remain in the family house on Silk Road. Her conscience had not allowed her to accept the palatial home recently vacated by the unfortunate Law Lord who'd met such a tragic death.

Talya wasn't sure if she'd ever want to live in that particular home anyway, bearing in mind the fate of its previous owner. How could she acquire affluence and prosperity when she'd seen for herself how much poverty and misery there was in The Climbs? Her power was in her position. She didn't need more wealth. She would have preferred to be able to share some of her good fortune with the people in The Climbs.

She'd become a Law Lord because it was the only way that she could influence legal affairs. She understood that she'd have to do things that she didn't like, challenges would have to be faced one at a time. But sure as hell, nothing was changing in The City if someone didn't have the guts to fight it from inside. The injustices would go on whether she was a Law Lord or not. Sooner be one of them, even if she was outnumbered, and try to figure it out and end it.

Talya knew that she'd need resilience and steadfastness that she'd never required before, but she was sure she had the stomach for whatever lay ahead. She might not have been quite so confident if she'd known that one of the first people to stand before her would be her own daughter.

CHAPTER FIVE

Salvage

Having to remove Jay's crushed skull from the pipework was one of the lower points of Max's work operating and maintaining the cleaner bots. He'd never come face-to-face with a victim before, most of the time he could detach himself from what was going on in there. Max had to go into his tool drawer to get something sturdy enough to lever out the jammed remains.

Jay's bloodied eyeball stared at him accusingly. He had to rush to his bin to throw up. Max hadn't got a weak stomach, but this was testing even him. He pulled, levered and eventually cajoled the blockage out of the mouth of the pipe. It rolled across the floor when it finally came free.

Max picked up the skull and felt compelled to acknowledge this man who'd fought so bravely in The Grid. He took a few moments in silence to pay his respects to Jay, then did what he had to do. He tossed the fleshy skull into the Bio-Shredder and it was devoured in a moment. There was no grave for those who sought and failed to gain justice – marked graves might have given cause for martyrdom.

As Max went to re-attach the pipe, he noticed something else, it was man-made and wrapped in the remains of a pouch. Whatever it was had been trapped by the skull. It would have been small enough to pass through had there not been a larger obstruction. It was bloody in there, so he hooked the remains out with one of his tools, rinsing it in water. As the human debris washed away from the object, it became clear what he was holding. It was a WristCom.

Max had never had direct access to one of these before. How had one got into The Grid? WristComs were usually worn by executive workers and more affluent Silk Roaders, certainly nobody at his pay grade ever got near one. It must have come in with one of the Justice Seekers – the only way they'd have got it through was inside their body, anything outside would be detected by security.

He cleaned away the final stains of blood and examined the unit carefully. There was a name etched onto the metallic disk at the back of it. Max's eyesight was poor, but he strained to read it. There was a T in there certainly, it was somebody's initials, it appeared to be a TS. There was a Fortrillium logo on it too – that figured, everybody at Fortrillium used these devices.

None of it meant much to Max, but somehow this WristCom had made its way into The Grid, and nobody knew about it. If Max was careful he could use the thing himself, it would go undetected. Okay, it was risky, but he was left on his own down there, it was just him and the bots. He was as certain as he could be that he could get away with it.

So Max concealed the device in a bag attached securely inside one of the outlet pipes of the cleaner bots, there was no way anybody else was going to find it there. He had a plan, but it would take some time and courage to work it through. Those WristComs were audio and digital devices, he knew enough about them from the screens to know that you could record video on them. They were mostly used for remote conferences and routine communications, but he had another purpose in mind.

Max was planning to send the WristCom in with the bots along the long tunnel to the centre of The Grid. He wanted to know what was in there.

Detection

Joe and Lucy considered the situation in the darkness of the sewer. Was there enough time for Lucy to make a run for it? They thought not.

Everybody in The City was chipped. At 20:00 there would be a location-based head count, anybody who was caught on the wrong side would be in trouble. This was to protect the Silk Roaders, though it had more to do with the control of crime under cover of darkness. It was also safety related. The Climbs were largely left to their own devices after dark. No Silk Roader would have volunteered to stay there at night, not even people like Lucy and Talya who were familiar faces to the residents. In the daytime you were protected by the many honest people in The Climbs, but in the darkness, when they were safely sheltering in their homes, there was nobody to keep you alive.

'Damn it!' cursed Lucy. 'Why wasn't Mitchell here to provide surveillance for us?'

Mitchell had a WristCom, as did Lucy, but she had been so absorbed among the wires that she'd neglected to watch the clock. Wiz had no such luxury, no residents in

The Climbs had WristCom access – unless they'd stolen one or cut off somebody's hand to get it.

'We need to get Mitchell up on your WristCom, Lucy. He'll need to stall for you.'

They pushed the wires back up into the void in the sewer pipe and quickly made their way to the end. Wiz checked that the coast was clear and they emerged from the hole in the ground, being careful to replace the drain cover so as not to arouse any suspicion. Lucy touched her WristCom and Mitchell responded almost immediately.

'Are you somewhere private?' asked Lucy.

'Yes, good to go,' came the reply. 'You alright?'

'I'm about to miss Segregation, Mitch. Can you create a clone for me?'

'Hell, Lucy, a bit more warning would be helpful. Quick, give me your access info.'

Lucy could hear Mitchell tapping away at his console, it was at a frantic speed.

'Okay. Slater-L,' she began. 'Zero, zero, five, alpha, gamma, gamma, two, nine, seven ...'

'Slower, slower. I'm writing a code base here and typing in your numbers. Start again from nine ...'

Lucy continued reading the digits from the tattoo on her left forearm. The tattoo was directly linked to a chip beneath the skin, it provided a unique identifier for everybody in The City.

'Okay,' said Mitchell, his brain in overdrive figuring out what he'd need to do to cheat the system.

Roll call was a wireless and momentary process. When it was triggered at Fortrillium, every device would be polled at rapid speed in alphabetical order. Mitchell's surname was Cranshaw, he would be counted in before Lucy, so that at least gave him warning when registration had begun.

'Ask Wiz, what's the best environment to place this in, SimBio or Vantrex?'

'SimBio,' Wiz replied straight away. 'Lucy, send him your Gen-ID.'

At rapid speed, Mitchell was creating a simulated biological framework into which he was going to place a virtual chip. He was going to cheat the chip into thinking it was embedded in Lucy, that's why he needed the DNA information. His own chip pulsed – he wouldn't have even noticed it under normal circumstances, but this time he was looking for it.

'We've got about three minutes, Lucy,' he said, still typing furiously away.

'When I say so, get down the sewer so you don't get polled twice. It should block the signal down there.'

A stream of digital information ran across Mitchell's display. It felt like ages to him, but in reality it was no more than half a minute. His terminal confirmed that the coding was accurate by correctly identifying as Slater, L. It looked as if it had worked. Mitchell swiped his hand across the screen, dropping a folder of data into the artificial environment that he'd just created.

'I reckon about sixty seconds,' came his voice on Lucy's WristCom. Get below ground now.'

'If you see your chip pulse, it didn't work. Good luck, I'll be waiting here, give it ten minutes before you come out.'

Wiz, Joe and Lucy went back down into the sewer, replacing the cover behind them.

'Go as far along the pipe as you can,' urged Joe. 'The deeper, the better.'

Joe and Lucy made their way through the duct. Wiz stayed at the entrance – he'd only hinder them. When they'd reached their usual place, just beneath the mess of wires where they'd abandoned work earlier, they sat in the darkness and waited. It was difficult to judge the time. Mitchell had said a minute.

Lucy held out her arm, they'd see the pulse if it happened. They stood by, hardly daring to blink unless they missed the momentary beat. Joe realized that he hadn't been exhaling, he tried to relax. They felt as if they'd been down there for hours, but it was only about fifteen minutes. Both were sure that the chip hadn't pulsed. They were ready to return to the surface to confirm with Mitchell.

Mitchell had only just begun breathing properly. He was good with tech, but it helped to get some thinking time. He was sweating, his forehead and back wet from the stress of what had just happened. Lucy's WristCom was active again, he heard her voice.

'Are we okay, Mitch?' she asked, hardly daring to hear the answer.

'It was fine,' came the reply. 'You're all accounted for in the system, nobody will know you're there tonight.'

Lucy relaxed now. She smiled at Joe and Wiz.

'Can you get a message to Mum, tell her I'm staying with the Parsons family overnight, say not to worry, I'll be back immediately after Segregation.'

'No problem, I'll make sure she knows ...'

Mitchell's voice stopped, as if he were deciding whether to say something or not. Lucy helped him. 'What?' she asked.

'I have got some bad news, I'm afraid. I don't know what time they'll do the morning poll, and they might do a spot check at any time of night. I can leave my console running so when they survey they'll track you to Silk Road.'

Lucy and Joe knew what he was going to say before he even said it.

'I'm sorry, Lucy, but the only safe way to guarantee not getting caught out is to stay down the sewer all night.'

Courted

Hannah had tried to make contact with Lucy to arrange a meeting, but her WristCom was either engaged or out of range. Unusual, but she was probably busy. Damien Hunter had said that he was on his way to some event involving Lucy's mum, so it was possible that she'd got caught up in it.

She couldn't believe the conversation that she'd just had. Everybody had their suspicions about the Gridder Games, but this was beyond what anyone could have imagined. There was no way she could discuss this with others outside her closest circle. Hunter had made it perfectly clear that if the information were shared a severe punishment would be given to the person leaking it and those receiving it. She didn't recall reading that bit in the contract that she'd signed, probably that's what you'd call 'small print'.

Hunter had explained to Hannah how the most capable Gridders were pro-actively courted by Fortrillium. Indeed, it was Fortrillium which secretly sponsored the contest. 'Think of it as a job interview,' he'd said. Fortrillium used the competition to isolate the best gamers, using computer-generated scenarios from previous Justice Trials.

'We're looking for skill, strategy, dexterity, and the ability to win at all costs,' he'd gone on to explain. 'You stood out, Hannah because you have an ability to anticipate Justice Seeker moves many steps ahead – I've never seen anything quite like it.'

Hannah resisted the urge to feel flattered by his

comments. She knew she was a skilled gamer, but that wasn't what all of this was about.

'Tomorrow morning I'd like you to report to Fortrillium, where you'll be inducted into the team which creates The Justice Trials. Your current job detail will be terminated, I'll handle that, and you start work for me at 08.00. Do you have any queries?'

Hannah had many questions that she'd like to ask, such as, 'How do The Grid trials operate?' and 'What happens if a Justice Seeker makes it through their trial?' She also wanted to know if she would ever be required to make a kill directly. She thought that they wouldn't let her loose on a trial for some time; she was banking on Lucy and Joe hacking into Fortrillium before that even became an issue. They needed to bring down Fortrillium before she was forced into taking a life – she'd have to step aside if it ever came to that. But could you hand in your resignation at Fortrillium? She wasn't so sure about that. They had to be successful in their attempts to infiltrate Fortrillium, they were all in too deep now. Failure could only mean disaster for all of them.

Hannah stuck with a benign question – she'd pick up the rest as she went along.

'I always wondered how the environments were rendered,' she began. 'Are they built or generated?'

That was safe and generalized, it didn't force Hunter into uncomfortable territory.

'They use pre-plague technology, it's ingenious. You create complete immersion scenarios on your console and we render those within The Grid. The Grid itself is a restricted space; using the system, it can feel infinite to the participants. They're effectively going over the same ground time and time again, but they can't tell, the environment changes infinitely as they move through the challenges.'

Hannah was intrigued. She was afraid and nervous, yet the gamer in her still wanted to know how it all worked.

'Other than the need for secrecy, are there any other key requirements for the position?'

Damien smiled at her and paused a moment.

'Yes,' he replied. 'There's just one. Nobody ever gets out of there. That's your job, you make sure that no-one ever leaves there alive.'

Clash

Talya worked her away around the room, exchanging pleasantries with her new colleagues from the panel of Law Lords. It wasn't an agreeable way to spend an evening, but she knew that she would have to grin and bear it. From now on she'd be seeing a lot of these people. The thing that surprised her was the wealth that was on display. Normally she mixed in much less ostentatious circles, but this was something new to her.

The majority of people living on Silk Road had the decency not to make a big fuss of the privilege that they were fortunate enough to enjoy. Most wouldn't openly acknowledge what was going on at the heart of their community in The Climbs, because they knew that their own lives and the lives of the people who lived there were precariously balanced. A small slip, a wrongly placed comment, making an enemy at Fortrillium, and your cosy life could come tumbling down in an instant. All it took was a knock at the door from the Centuria – if you were lucky enough to be afforded that courtesy.

In spite of watching their own backs, they knew what

was going on over in The Climbs. Even if they'd never had the courage to cross over, there was always the gnawing feeling of guilt and discomfort. They knew that their good fortune brought misery and squalor for others. What could you do if you had families to care for? Nobody would volunteer for The Climbs; you just had to shelter your immediate dependents and be thankful that your own lot was a good one.

There was no such shame from the Law Lords. Their dominant position in society made them almost untouchable, they were given the highest privileges and a level of prosperity enjoyed by nobody else in The City. This was what also agitated President Delman – this wealth did not automatically come with the job, yet he too was aware of how much affluence was on display. He would never have been able to prove it, but he knew it was Hunter's doing. Fortrillium controlled law and order in The City. Sure, the President was involved with policy, but it was what they referred to as 'arm's length' service. That meant Damien Hunter ran it and there was not a lot the President could do to change it, not while Hunter had bought the allegiance of those serving within the justice system.

It was a stalemate, that's why Delman had brought in Talya. She was a liability, but she was completely straight and honest. It had taken him a long time to find somebody with the correct legal background who was also incorruptible. People like Talya were rare in The City – she seemed to have a death wish in that she would not step back from saying and doing the right thing. Of course, this made her a problem. She'd even dared to criticize the President while appearing on the screens, but he desperately needed someone like her, particularly with what was coming.

President Delman could feel the long, wiry tentacles of

Fortrillium circling around him. He knew what Damien Hunter was after and what that would eventually mean for him. His leadership had been sustained and unchallenged for many years. However, Hunter was like nobody else he'd ever encountered. His ability to intimidate, control, corrupt and – if necessary – charm, was unstoppable, he was slowly colonizing all of the President's supporters. The endgame would be that Delman was isolated – an ageing President would be unable to fight off the major challenge.

President Delman knew that he was hanging on by a thread, but he didn't need to maintain this position for much longer. He hadn't become President by being passive. Bringing Talya in was his masterstroke; with her in place he would be able to separate the fact from the fiction. He watched her making her way around the room, the only member of the justice panel not to be dripping in jewellery or wearing a diamond-encrusted WristCom.

Damien Hunter arrived, late, but instantly dominating the room with his entrance. Talya hadn't noticed him imme-diately, as she was reading a text message from Lucy's friend Mitchell when he arrived. Her daughter had got caught in The Climbs. Talya knew she'd be safe there with Joe, but she couldn't help but worry about how they'd evaded detection after Segregation. She had to trust Lucy, she knew she was capable and streetwise, but that didn't stop the panic rising in her.

Talya checked herself. She'd have to get used to feeling one thing and showing another. She was in a room with the two most influential men in The City. Both of them had the power to sentence Lucy to incarceration for the rest of her life, it would barely matter that she was a Law Lord now.

Damien Hunter soon edged in on her conversation,

effectively blanking out the person that she'd been speaking to and dismissing them, without even a word.

'Congratulations, Talya, I'm delighted that you're now joining us on the panel, it's well deserved.'

He'd barely drawn breath and he was lying already. Firstly she knew for a fact that he'd been leaning on Delman not to appoint her, probably trying to dig up all sorts of scandal to block it. Secondly, the use of 'us' was instantly telling. There was no 'us' when it came to justice within The City, the Law Lords were the final power. Fortrillium's role was to deliver their will – it was not supposed to be the other way round.

'Thank you, Damien,' Talya replied, mustering every bit of charm that she could. 'It's an absolute privilege to be able to serve The City.'

Okay, she was lying now too. She thought of the office more like a poisoned chalice, but there was no way she was sharing those thoughts in public.

'Of course, you understand that we'll be working closely together now, Talya, and I do hope that you'll impress upon your child – Lucy is it? – the responsibilities that come with your new role.'

This man was unbelievable. Here was the veiled threat already. Translate that last sentence in Hunter speak and she'd just been told to watch herself: Damien Hunter was monitoring Talya and her daughter. It had begun immediately. If she were a weaker person, she'd be next in line for the massive house and gaudy jewellery. No doubt this is how he'd intimidated every one of the other members of the panel, by letting them know that their families were in danger if they didn't work with him.

Talya felt the panic rise in her once again. If Hunter knew where Lucy was, it would be the shortest Law Lord appointment in history. They'd have to have words. Lucy needed to be aware that they'd be watching carefully from now on.

'Of course, Damien. Lucy is more concerned with building a career for herself in network forensics these days. She hopes that she can join Fortrillium in future years, it certainly seems to be her aspiration.'

Another lie, how many would she be forced to tell? Lucy was more likely to blow up Fortrillium than work for it – she'd never stopped blaming them for her father's disappearance. Fortunately for Talya, even she didn't know what Lucy was up to: hacking into Fortrillium's networked infrastructure. Not quite the career choice that they'd discussed.

Talya decided to take the initiative. If Hunter was throwing down the gauntlet so soon, she'd have to move fast to outmanoeuvre him. An early advantage would help her to secure her own leverage.

'As you know, Damien, the new role affords me certain non-civilian privileges, and I'd like to move on these swiftly.'

Damien Hunter's face changed from its forced charm to a more natural scowl.

'I'd like to request a tour of the detention facilities operated by Fortrillium so that I can be more informed in my new role.'

Few people ever got to see The Soak, only Fortrillium employees who were sworn to secrecy, and those who entered it and never left. Most Law Lords gave it a wide berth; they all knew about it, but none of them wanted to acknowledge its existence.

'No problem at all.' Damien's charming face returned, though it took a little more effort to get it in place this time.

'That's quite difficult to arrange. I'm sure that we can organize that for you within, say, the next year – is that a reasonable time frame for you?'

'No, it's not,' replied Talya. She'd been expecting a stall from him.

'As you know, under article IP6.v3 Law Lords have the right to inspect all detention facilities at one hour's notice.'

Damien's scowl was back. It was proving too much for him to even pretend charm now.

'I want to have a full tour at 08:00 tomorrow Damien, so I'm being generous, you've got almost twelve hours warning.'

'No problem at all Talya, I'll get that arranged for you straight away.

'By the way, how is that daughter of yours?'

CHAPTER SIX

Jay

Jay reached the highest floor, bent over and placed his hands on his knees to steady himself. It had taken him seven minutes, bottom to top, and he was exhausted. There weren't a lot of advantages to living in The Climbs, but you could certainly keep yourself fit here – if you could find enough food that was.

Jay was a runner for his block. It wasn't a remunerated job, but those in The Climbs who did have compensated work shared what they had with people like Jay because he provided a valuable service.

People living in The Climbs weren't paid with money, they received tokens for food and clothing. Water was made available via large butts placed on every street corner, and if you were lucky they were kept full.

As one of the youngest and fittest in The Climbs, people like Jay were obvious choices for runners. From 06:00 until 20:00, curfew time, he would deliver water and food supplies all over his block. There was no piped water here, that was for Silk Road residents only. People in The Climbs had to wash and drink using supplies from the huge public tanks. Showers and baths didn't exist. There were remnants of bathrooms from before the plague, some had lashed up shower-like devices from old parts, but they weren't plumbed in anywhere, the only water available was the water from the butts.

Jay kept himself fit this way. He was strong and healthy. He was paid in food tokens by the people in his block and he was used to carrying the large plastic bottles on his shoulders as he ran up and down the stairs. He was popular too, why wouldn't he be? Jay's activities were keeping people alive.

Jay had never been in trouble with the Centuria before. His life had been as uneventful as it could be in The Climbs. The odd scrape here and there, but nothing to attract the attention of the authorities. That's why it had taken him aback when the visit came six years ago. He'd had a lot of time to think about it sitting in his cage in The Soak, and he was never sure if he was chosen or if he just got unlucky. Wrong time, wrong place perhaps?

He was quite young at the time, he'd lost track of his age, but supposed he must have been about eighteen when it happened. It was just before curfew, and he was about to make a final run to the water butt; this one was the last trip of the day, it was for him and his mum. They lived ten floors up, not too high, he'd be back in plenty of time for curfew.

As he approached the water butt, a man walked up to him and put a hand on his shoulder.

'Look up to your level,' he said, no introductions.

The voice was familiar, but the man had taken some cursory trouble to disguise his appearance. Jay couldn't place him

He wasn't quite sure what to do, it was immediately unsettling. He glanced up to the tenth floor, it was just low enough to see what was going on. He flinched, and his automatic reaction was to threaten the man at his side.

'Steady,' he said, holding Jay's arm which was raised and ready to strike.

'What's this about? Don't you hurt her!' shouted Jay.

He glanced back up at his mum. She was being dangled out of the window of her apartment by two men – they didn't appear to be Centuria from that distance, he couldn't be sure. They each had one arm, and she'd got something over her mouth so she couldn't scream.

'No need to hurt her if you play nice,' said the man. His calmness suggested that he was accustomed to this level of casual violence.

'I want you to step into this vehicle.'

He signaled towards the black van parked along the street. Jay had noticed it earlier on his water runs, but he'd thought little of it. You didn't see many vehicles in The Climbs, but this one seemed to be harmless, on city business he'd reckoned.

'What if I don't?' challenged Jay.

The man lifted his right hand as a signal and ten floors above them one of the men released the limb that he was holding.

Jay's mum began to struggle, she was being held by just one arm.

'Okay, okay, just make sure Mum's safe. You bring her inside the window and I'll do what you've asked.'

'No, it's not going to work that way,' came the reply. 'We'll hold her by two arms and you'll do what I say.'

He gestured to the man above them, and once again Jay's mother was grasped more securely. Jay walked towards the van, fearful as to what was going to happen next. He had no options here, he had to comply.

The interior of the vehicle had been converted for medical purposes, and Jay was guided to lie on a metal table and extend his arm. He was surrounded by equipment, the like of which they didn't have access to in The Climbs. Instinct told him what was about to happen next would not be good.

The man who'd threatened him watched – this was going to be carried out by the woman who'd been concealed in the van.

'We're going to place something in your arm,' said the man. 'It's going to hurt, but it will heal. You will never speak of this. If anybody asks, the wound came from a fall on the stairs.

'You will leave this device where we place it. If you fail to comply your mother will die.

'Understood?'

The woman made an incision in Jay's forearm, just above his chip, and he flinched.

'Understood?' demanded the man, as if nothing had happened.

'Yes, yes, understood!' Jay winced through the pain.

The woman drove a small circular object into a BioPouch, then forced the package into the flesh which she'd just exposed with her scalpel. Jay recognized the item as a WristCom; he'd seen them on the screens, but never actually handled one. The pouch was entirely alien to him, but essential to the man who was standing at his side. The BioPouch would screen it from detection in any security scans, it would be hidden and secure.

The woman removed her fingers from Jay's flesh and pushed the two sides of the laceration together. With no care to avoid discomfort, she quickly stitched up Jay's arm and placed a bandage on the raw wound.

'Remember, you fell on the stairs,' said the man. 'Never show the stitches, never tell anybody what happened here today, never remove the device.'

'Okay, I get it,' said Jay, desperate to get out of the van and check on his mum.

He was finally released and relieved to see that his mother was no longer dangling from the window.

Jay never knew what had occurred on that night, but his survival instincts told him that he needed to keep this to himself. These people meant business, you didn't mess with the authorities or whoever it was who'd done this to him.

'Thank you, Susan,' the man said to the medic as Jay made his way back towards his tower block. 'That bit of evidence will be safe there if we ever need it again.'

She smiled a collusive smile. He wouldn't usually bother to explain himself to a subordinate, but to preserve the trail of secrecy he'd be disposing of her in the next five minutes anyway. Never leave footprints, that was his rule. This item of evidence might be needed later. Always remove witnesses.

Susan, who hadn't yet realized that this was a one-time job with no pension at the end of it, went about clearing up the van.

'No problem at all, any time I can be of assistance. It's always a pleasure to serve The City, President Delman.'

Intervention

Reevil96 switched off his console and slammed his fist on the desk. It was getting more and more difficult to defend the core. The systems and procedures that they'd put in place were supposed to protect their greatest secret, but the Gridders seemed to be becoming weaker, the gameplay sloppier. The Justice Seekers were becoming stronger and more resourceful.

He'd had to intervene once again when the Justice Seeker known as Jay had got so near to the core. If the population of The City had realized how close he was, what they were looking at on their screens, there might have been riots. That would have been the first time that it had ever happened within its high walls. The ecosystem of rich, poor and an iron hand had kept things in a perfect equilibrium for many years since the plague. But if the secret were ever revealed, if the truth ever became known? Well, it would all crumble around them fast.

Reevil96 picked up the new files on Hannah; they'd just been sent securely to his console. He scanned her reaction times, checked the strategic scores and surveyed her psychometric profile. She seemed highly suitable on paper, but something was not ringing true to him.

Reevil96 was the Master Gridder, though nobody at Fortrillium knew it. He was in sole charge of ensuring that nobody ever made it as far as The Justice Walk. The cards were always stacked against the Justice Seekers, there was never any chance of them making it out of there alive. The entire process had been constructed for protection and defence. The Grid served as a big electrified fence that nobody was ever meant to pass through.

Hannah was fresh blood, a new member of the team. He would never get to meet her, the Gridders didn't even know of his existence, but they must have suspected. He'd had to intervene at the last moment with Jay, he couldn't let it go on any longer, he was sure that Jay was going to make it to the core.

In the final minutes, he'd taken over control of the game-play. He'd come up with an obstacle that Jay simply didn't have the energy to take on, and finished him off in no time at all. Jay never stood a chance, but the Gridders should have seen it coming. They thought they'd beaten Jay with their final play, but he was quick and intelligent, he cheated them and they were caught out, they had nothing left to throw at him. Reevil96 had jumped in fast, taking control of The Grid via his own console, re-rendering the environment at incredible speed, desperate to beat Jay. He'd been forced to kill again too, he despised himself for that.

Unknown to him, his interference had been detected by two teenagers concealed within a sewage pipe in the poorest part of The City. They'd identified a cable infrastructure that nobody inside The City should have been aware of, yet they'd discovered that second source, a glimpse of something else that might be controlling their destiny. Although they were unaware of it at the time, Joe and Lucy had spied their Nemesis in that dark, stinking tunnel, the man who would hold their fate in his hands within the next three days.

But Reevil96 had spotted something in Hannah's files, his suspicions had been aroused, he was not the Master Gridder without a very good reason. He could spot a game-play from several steps back. Hannah James had gamed the system, she'd used a series of ingenious strategies and cheats to guide her way to the winning position. He was on to her and he'd be watching when she made her move.

Atrocity

Damien was angry. Talya had got him wound up. Every Law Lord he'd ever known had declined the right to check out Fortrillium's facilities. One or two had asked, but a brief reference to family members or a mention of some sensitive information that they might prefer to stay private, and most accepted his offer of a visit within a year. That never happened, of course, it was conveniently forgotten about and the Law Lord didn't mention it again – especially after the intimidation was promptly followed up by a gift the following day. Law Lords soon learned that it was better to take 'guidance' from Damien Hunter – rewards for good behaviour would always follow swiftly afterwards.

He'd always found the Law Lords so easy to control, but he knew he had a job on his hands with Talya Slater. What had Delman been thinking about appointing her? She was going to be a pain to both of them. As someone commanding more public support than the two of them put together, Talya's little moral crusades were becoming a threat to the status quo.

You would think what happened to her husband would have scared her off, but it seemed to invigorate her. He'd watched her climb from grieving widow and mother to respected lawyer, influential citizen and screen celebrity. People warmed to her, and that was always going to be a problem.

If he and Delman had one thing in common, it was that The City had no choice about them – they were stuck with them, whether they liked it or not. Everybody was too fearful to make a challenge, the system was perfectly balanced to keep them in their respective offices.

But Talya Slater didn't follow the rules, it seemed that she couldn't be bought or intimidated. Delman had been canny, moving her so close to him. If he hadn't been quite so spiteful, Damien might have thought of that one, but he'd missed his chance.

No worries, Talya was not immune, he'd shake her up with a threat to her child – she was a teenager, bound to be up to something. Her files had already raised some interesting movements in The Climbs, no doubt a relationship with Parsons. A lovely bit of scandal for a Law Lord that, a daughter seeing someone in The Climbs, he'd be able to turn that into something threatening to Talya.

He'd contacted the office and Talya's visit was all arranged. She'd see what she needed to see and the problem would soon go away. They'd steer her away from the important areas, she'd be in and out of there in no time. A quick threat to Lucy's activities, followed by a financial sweetener and she'd toe the line. They all did eventually, and if not? Well, it was unbelievable how dangerous The City could be at times.

Still, no need to carry the stress around with him all night. That was why he was in The Climbs. No Segregation for the Head of Fortrillium, for him The City had no areas that were out of bounds. This was where he came whenever he needed to let off steam.

There were always homeless people in this area. Those who'd not managed to find vacant living quarters in one of the tower blocks, or who had been forced onto the streets because infirmity or disability had meant that they could no longer manage the stairs. It was the chance of food scraps and survival on the pavements, or certain death in a cramped, dirty apartment high above the ground.

Damien hated the untidiness of it all. He despised the homeless inhabitants of The Climbs, looking down on them as the weakest and most needy in their small world.

'File a news report about an unfortunate massacre in The Square, suspect escaped, no witnesses, twelve dead, Centuria investigating.'

The man at his side nodded, pulling out a console and beginning to type as instructed. He was used to this, reporting a news story which hadn't yet happened.

Damien reached into the black car and bought out a weapon. He aimed it at the closest homeless person to him, who was asleep under a threadbare blanket, leaning against a wall. He fired. The man's body jumped and then was still, a pool of blood forming around his head. Damien shot again. A woman this time, with her two children, another man, running to escape the carnage. It was too easy.

The shots rang out for five minutes as Damien Hunter chose his victims one by one.

When The Square was quiet and littered with fresh corpses, he handed the gun to one of the Centuria at his side.

He turned to the man who was filing the story for the screens: 'Update that report, it needs to say nineteen dead.'

Connected

A night in the sewer, it wasn't their idea of fun, but at least Mitchell had saved Lucy from detection. They weren't out of trouble yet, they had to avoid discovery until Segregation ended at 06:00. It was going to be a long night for both of them. For Joe, it was a night spent among the rats, for Lucy, being caught there could mean disaster. She hoped that Mitchell had managed to alert her mum, all she needed now was some missing person hunt started by an anxious Talya. Mitchell had been amazing so far, she was sure he wouldn't let them down.

Joe sent Wiz back home – he was so tall, he'd have been unable to walk for a week if he had to spend a night down in the sewer.

'Make sure you don't get spotted out after curfew,' warned Joe, 'but get a message to my mum that I'm okay.'

Wiz lived in a block that was very close to Joe's. It's how they'd become friends; he was used to moving around after curfew, he'd be fine.

'Hey, and get back here as soon as you can after 06:00!' shouted Lucy. 'I have to get home as quickly as I can.'

She'd need to leave via a different gate, she didn't want to arouse suspicion with the Centuria. Probably best to clean up at Joe's, and then head out of The Climbs a little later, it would be suspicious leaving so early in the morning.

'We might as well carry on working,' said Joe. 'The more I have to focus on, the less I'll think about the rats.'

'Can we do it without Wiz and Mitchell?' asked Lucy.

Joe was sure that they could. They'd secured access a few nights previously using Wiz's codes, the rest was a job for Joe. Lucy's skills would be needed once they were in.

'Have you heard from Hannah?' asked Joe. 'How did she get on in the Gridder Games?'

'I can't tell yet, I have messages from her, but I can't connect down here.'

It would have to wait for now. Hannah's performance in the Gridder Games had been in their minds all day, but there was nothing they could do about it at that moment. Hannah's success in the contest would be the final part of their plan coming to fruition.

Joe grabbed the wires that they'd hurriedly concealed at the top of the pipework; they had to be careful to keep them dry, they could lose a couple of nights' work if the cables got damp. Between them, they manipulated each wire into place.

'Will the power last the night?'

'Not sure, I've never used it this long before.'

'Okay, we're live. Let's enter the codes and we're back where we were the other night.'

Joe entered the information and the console displayed the screen view that they'd succeeded in bringing up previously. They'd managed to prove that there was more than one data source alongside Fortrillium, but they still couldn't get into either of them. The chances of ever getting into the external source were minimal; they had no information on which to base a hack. It was interesting, though, as they had always understood that all data was carried through Fortrillium's network. The discovery of the other night had suggested that wasn't true.

'We need to ignore that location for now and focus on the Fortrillium network. What do you think?'

Lucy analyzed the digital sequences on the screens. She'd seen this before at work, that configuration was familiar. Fresh eyes and a break of a few days had allowed her to approach the problem anew.

'Let me try something,' she said, leaning across Joe to take the console. The pair were so accustomed to each other that there was no awkwardness as she leaned over and pressed against his arm. Joe let her take it, he was a bit out of his depth. Lucy typed away, it was so hard to work with only the light of the screen.

Alone down there in the darkness, Joe imagined the rats that must be all around them in the sewer; he had to use all the willpower that he could muster to fight his fear. He thought of Zach and hoped he'd be okay with the provisions that he'd left. Joe had expected to call in on him that evening, that wouldn't be happening after recent events.

'Look at this, I'm in,' Lucy announced in the darkness. 'It's quite straightforward, I'm surprised that there's not more protection there.'

Joe suspected that it was probably because there was nobody who would even dare think about doing what they were doing. If everybody is terrified of you, it's fine to leave your front door open.

Lucy typed frantically at the screen, and Joe watched. He was able to follow what she was up to, he wanted to learn this for himself. If he'd stayed on Silk Road he would have chosen a similar career path to Lucy.

'Can you try the data card? You did bring it with you, I hope?'

Of course he had. Joe was never parted from the device, it was all he had left of his dad. He kept it with him as a constant reminder of his mission, to find out who'd had their fathers killed – and why. He inserted it into the console.

'Okay, you'll need to authenticate.'

Joe placed his finger on the panel; the authentication was completed. This was the bit only he could do – the data was encrypted for family use, they'd done this before, but never while connected to the Fortrillium network. Last time they got to this stage it ended in disappointment. They got to his dad's stored information, but they couldn't read it off a conventional system.

'This is encouraging,' said Lucy. 'See, it's reading the device, it recognizes the file types.'

Sure enough, the encrypted information on Matt's card was being deciphered right there on the screen.

Seventy percent complete ... eighty-three percent complete ... ninety-two percent complete ... then it reached one hundred percent. They'd waited six years for this, they were going to get answers at last.

Without warning, just as the progress bar indicated completion, there was darkness. The console faded to black. They'd run out of power – they'd had the explanation at their fingertips, only to be blocked at the last minute.

'You're kidding!' Joe snapped in the blackness. He felt something brush by his feet, a rat; he was too frustrated to react at that moment, his mind fixed on their dilemma.

'No, surely not?' said Lucy.

She set straight to work, trying to solve the problem. It was tricky in the dark tunnel, their console had provided the light for them to continue.

'Can we take a charge from your WristCom, and hop it through the battery unit?' suggested Joe. He wasn't hopeful. Not having a WristCom, he'd never had the chance to investigate one carefully. He knew that they self-generated their power from a combination of solar and body movement, using direct top-ups only occasionally.

'I'm onto it,' Lucy replied. 'We need to be careful not to take it offline – if we do I'll risk getting flagged on the register, and everything that Mitchell did will have been a waste of time.'

Making the most of the small light from the WristCom, Joe and Lucy worked swiftly with the synchronized movements of people who were accustomed to working well together. A redeployment of wires and a quick reconfiguration of the power source and the console lit up once again. They were in.

'We don't have much time to do this, we must keep some charge in my WristCom. It's only used kinetic charging while we've been in the dark, there's not a lot of juice left in it.'

'No problem, let's dig deeper on this framework, there must be something here that we can use.'

The pair worked adeptly, Joe deferring to Lucy, who recognized the network protocols immediately. They could finally read Matt's card data. It was a jumble of jottings, images, video files and observations. Joe scanned it at speed while Lucy attended to gaining access.

'It's notes about Damien Hunter and Fortrillium,' Joe began, summarizing. 'It confirms what we thought; there is a second source – your dad was in on it, it's what they were investigating when they died.'

Joe was always surprised at how matter of fact they could be about the deaths of their fathers. They'd talked about this so much that it had almost become somebody else's story. It was only when alone at night that he would burn with anger and frustration. When they were down there in the sewers, working to solve the problem, he felt that he'd taken some power back.

'They knew that Hunter was onto them, there was something between him and the President going on, but they don't seem to know what it was all about. Dad mentions a lot of tension between them, struggles over authority and accusations – they don't hit it off by the sound of it.'

Lucy signaled for him to stop for a moment, and she took over the console and worked at the screen.

'We're right, there are two networks. They're entirely separate by default. One of them is Fortrillium, we know about that, but this second one is something completely different, it comes from an alternative source. The second network can join Fortrillium's via a gateway, but it's one way only, Fortrillium cannot reciprocate on the other network.'

Joe realized what she was saying. 'Which means that there's something more powerful than Fortrillium out there …'

'But it's not inside The City.' Lucy picked up his

sentence. 'It's different infrastructure, this is not like anything I've seen within The City.'

'What could outrank Fortrillium? The President's office?'

Joe switched back to his dad's notes. For him this was like discovering a long-lost diary, it was a chance to talk to the dead.

'There are comments about Hunter here, all sorts of incidents about him intimidating people – he added dates too. Dad reckons Hunter was killing people in The Climbs, says he was doing it for sport, there are pictures here somewhere.'

Joe fumbled around on the console; he was getting cramped and uncomfortable balanced against the cold curve of the sewer pipe. A folder of images appeared on the screen. Joe and Lucy didn't need to study it too closely, they could see immediately what they were. Image after image of Damien Hunter firing weapons, a leer of exhilaration on his face. Dead bodies on the ground, people running in terror. Joe closed the folder, he felt sick, he recognized some of the locations from The Climbs in the images.

He was frustrated. It felt as if they were no further forward. They knew there was a second stream, but they didn't know its source. He'd confirmed that his dad was onto something, that he had incriminating evidence which could put Damien Hunter in The Grid – that's if it ever saw the light of day. Who could they give that information to? It would be suppressed and they would meet the same fate as their fathers had. The discoveries were explosive, but what could they do with them?

The console screen dimmed and Lucy pulled out the wires.

'We have to leave it there, Joe, I can't risk my WristCom.'

They were annoyed with themselves, angry that they'd finally managed to break into Fortrillium's network and access Matt's data, but stopped dead in their tracks by a failing power source. They felt that the night had been risky and futile. Wiz would be back shortly. Lucy would need to re-enter Silk Road and it would be a few days until they risked entering the sewer again to re-establish the network connection.

They needn't have been frustrated if they'd known what was coming. The information that they'd secured on that night would become pivotal in surviving the horror that was to follow.

CHAPTER SEVEN

Forgotten

Harry was annoyed with herself. How could she have forgotten to mention that to Talya? She was such a lovely lady, so good to her, and she'd neglected a crucial piece of information that she should have passed on.

Harry stared out of her window. She couldn't see much from up there, just the other apartment windows looking in on the miserable lives of the inhabitants. The tower blocks had been luxurious once, some still contained broken remnants of the previous world, but it had been so long ago, everything was crumbling.

She thought back to her unusual life – the twins, David, where were they now? Had they survived the plague years? She didn't know, they'd been separated in the tunnels, it was all so long ago now. It happened fast, she was too young to know what was going on.

Harry had been stuck in the tower block for over twelve years, dependent on others to bring her provisions. There were not many who even cared about her stories. They'd all been cowed. She was one of the few who remembered, but even those few were so used to this new world that they were unsure what was real and what was just a fantasy. It was illegal to talk about the days before the plague; she had to be careful who she shared her memories with.

Harry sighed and began the slow walk across the room to the table where Talya had left the pills. Her hands were so stiff and painful, she'd need the tablets to help her sleep through the night – if the rats didn't wake her, she hated their scratching. Harry feared the creatures, they'd know when she died, they were waiting for her – a hearty meal once she'd taken her final breath.

That time must come soon. She was tired and lonely, the days were long and hard, there were not many visitors. She'd filled the time with her memories, but even they were beginning to fade. She could remember what she'd meant to tell Talya though, but she wouldn't see her again. Talya had tears in her eyes when she'd passed on the bad news, promising her daughter Lucy would bring supplies, but that she couldn't visit again.

Harry was tired. She would be ready when it came, even though she hated the thought of the rats getting to her before her body was discovered. It would soon be time to reunite with the others in death, to join the joy and companionship of the family that she missed so much. Her heart ached for those days, she'd never see them again, but she longed to hear the laughter once more. Had she appreciated it enough at the time, before the plague? She hoped so.

She'd have to hang on a little longer, though. She had to explain to Lucy what she'd forgotten to tell her mother. So sad for a girl to grow up without a father, but at least her mother was resilient, Harry knew how important it was to have a capable mother.

She thought about the President, and how she'd revealed to Talya the story about him surviving The Grid. She'd got her thoughts muddled and only given Talya part of the story. It was the strangest thing, it was so long ago. Josh Delman had been a young man at the time. Still, they'd all got a lot older. Not many people could remember, and those who could knew better than to share the information. She was right, Delman was the only person to have survived The Grid, but there was something else altogether unique about him.

Many people hadn't even noticed at the time. After a while the faces of the Justice Seekers became a blur, it could be hard to keep up with those who died. Sometimes they met their fates so fast in there. Delman was entirely different, though. Sure, he was the last person standing, he got to make The Justice Walk to freedom. The trouble was, nobody ever remembered him going in there in the first place. They all saw him exit The Grid, but not one person saw him enter. His arrival was a complete surprise, there was no one who knew where he'd come from.

The next thing they knew, he was their President.

Defiance

Talya was feeling shaky, it was unlike her. She was worried that Lucy had been out all night, and she'd have liked to have seen her before leaving for work that morning. Lucy didn't even know that her mother had been sworn in as a Law Lord, where was she?

Talya was unnerved, was it a coincidence that Lucy had

all but disappeared just as she'd become a Law Lord? Her WristCom was not receiving messages, the whole set up didn't feel right. She hoped that she hadn't done something rash or foolish accepting the new position, she'd never forgive herself if she'd put Lucy in danger.

She had to keep a straight face, continue moving forward, and assume that Lucy was okay. She'd have heard by now, surely?

She was soon distracted from her own problems, though. She had barely been sworn in and they already had a sitting of the Law Lords scheduled for 07:00 that morning. More inmates wanted to enter The Grid. Why did they do it, she wondered? Talya knew that this went on, how else did prisoners end up being killed on their screens? She had no taste for it, she'd never really watched closely since she'd had to witness Matt perish. Fortunately, she'd been spared the moment of his death, but she'd seen enough.

It was hard to keep her resolve and she could change nothing from the sidelines. She had to drink with the devil if anything was to be challenged or changed.

She'd been shocked by the perfunctoriness of it all, sitting up there above the inmates fully gowned and dominating, utterly unable to help them.

The first thing that had taken her aback was the state of the detainees. They were dirty, poorly clothed, some of them just skin and bone, they hadn't seen a good meal in ages. It had required a substantial exertion of will on her part not to throw up. She wasn't going to give Leianna Richwald that satisfaction as she smirked at her from her central position among the Law Lords.

What had shocked Talya most was the courage of the man called Clay. He still appeared healthy enough, the records showed that he'd only recently been detained. What had forced him to face inevitable death in The Grid? Why hadn't he tried to survive a little longer?

Nobody ever saw where the inmates were housed, it was purely a place for imagination and conjecture. Fortrillium preferred it that way. Now she was a Law Lord she would see for herself, it was the only chance she'd ever have to do so.

The process was new to her. They'd been seated before the inmates came into the courtroom. There was not a lot to indicate that it was a courtroom, just the Fortrillium emblem positioned on the wall behind the seven judges. They sat on their Seats of Justice, on a platform looking down on the prisoners.

They were herded into the room wearing electronic neck tags. Talya dare not even guess what they were for, she'd discover later on during her tour of the facilities no doubt – if Damien Hunter hadn't already covered up any incriminating trails, that is. She reckoned he'd be working on it as they sat in court, he'd probably arranged that morning's sitting as a delaying tactic.

It was Clay who spoke for the inmates, reading from a prepared statement.

'We here present demand the right to pursue justice under the laws of our city. As outlined in the Law of Retribution, we hereby request the right to seek a trial in The Grid, to be granted our freedom in The Justice Walk if our innocence is proved. Our collective crimes are theft, murder, deception, assault, forgery and misappropriation of provisions. Will you grant us our right?'

There was no consultation. 'Granted!' shouted Leianna Richwald.

Talya was caught off guard, they were supposed to question and consult at this stage.

'I challenge,' replied Talya, recovering her wits, but unable to stop her voice shaking.

There was silence. One by one the Law Lords turned to glare at her. Talya could feel their eyes boring into her, but she stared ahead, watching the man Clay who had just spoken.

'Which of you is guilty of the lesser crime of misappropriation of provisions?' she asked.

There were seven inmates, two of them indicated that they had been convicted of the minor infraction.

'Under City Law Section 5, 2b this crime is not covered by the Law of Retribution.'

The hostility towards Talya was almost tangible. Leianna Richwald inhaled sharply, even the prisoners seemed surprised at the challenge.

'Overruled,' she shouted. 'Those on trial may invoke their right for group justice, in which the crimes of the many are subsumed by all.

'The Justice Walk will be shared by those whose innocence is proved.'

The Centuria who were guarding the captives ushered them towards the exit. Clay drew breath, he'd been emboldened by the challenge that they'd just witnessed. Dissent was not something that people were used to in The City, most were too fearful to even try it.

'This whole process is a sham!' he began. 'I was only taking food to give to the sick and elderly—'

He was struck on the head by one of the Centuria. He fell to his knees but carried on.

'The conditions for inmates are unbearable, the cages filled with innocent people who are forced to suffer. I go to seek justice as an honest man but there is no justice in this—'

Clay was struck again and this time he dropped to the ground. The remaining detainees, shaken by what had just occurred, shuffled out of the courtroom towards the temporary holding area. Clay was carried out, there was a smear of blood where his head had been on the floor.

Talya tried to regulate her breathing, her heart thumped urgently, she was terrified at the violence that she'd just seen. The Law Lord to her right leaned over towards her and spoke. It was Law Lord Brad Sivil.

'Do not do that again, not if you want to live, he sees it all.'

'Who? Who sees it all?' replied Talya.

The Law Lord wouldn't be drawn. Talya got no answer to her question.

She'd just seen the law at work. And it stank.

Arrest

Jay had been relieved to find his mum alive and unharmed in the apartment. He didn't see his mother's assailants leaving the building on the way up the stairs, just as he hadn't seen them entering earlier as he'd delivered provisions throughout his block. There was more than one staircase, but they'd taken a lot of trouble over the surprise attack.

His arm was red and raw, he could feel where the incision had been made. What had they placed under his skin? Why had they chosen him? At that moment Jay was so scared he didn't care that much, he could only think of his mum. She was pale and gaunt, terrified by having been dangled out of the window of the apartment.

Jay did what he could to comfort her, and she finally settled down and rested on her old damp mattress.

That was the last of it for several years. The wound soon healed, it had been expertly cut, and Jay grew accustomed to the feeling of the WristCom beneath his flesh. Everybody knew better than to ask about the scar and life quickly returned to normal. Except that Jay's mum died not too long afterwards, she'd been severely shaken by the events of that violent day and never fully recovered. There was nothing that Jay could do about it. He'd been raging when his mother's body was taken away for disposal, but what could he do? There was nothing to do but to keep on with his running duties, to continue serving the people who needed him in his block, and stay off the radar of the Centuria. It was all any of them could do, to survive.

After the pain of his mother's death had subsided, and the scar long since healed, Jay had pushed those events to the back of his mind. Most days would pass without his thinking about what had happened. Until his life took an abrupt turn.

He was nearing the end of another day running up and down the stairs of the tower block when a black car drove past. The images of that day six years ago came straight back to haunt him. The car passed by, but a sight like this was unusual in The Climbs, he knew that it would be connected.

A few minutes passed, and the car came around again. This time Jay knew it was him. He actually walked up to the vehicle as it slowed down just ahead of him.

The window wound down. Jay recognized the face, but it was not who he expected it to be. Damien Hunter spoke to him.

'You're Jay Morgan?' he asked.

Jay nodded.

'You know this woman?' he asked, holding up an image.

It was a picture of the woman who'd performed the surgery on Jay's arm. He tried not to give the game away, but he knew as soon as he attempted the deceit that Damien had seen it on his face. Hunter wound up his window and drove off.

Jay was terrified. It would have been better if Hunter had confronted him there and then. Driving off like that, it felt even more intimidating somehow.

He was on edge for the following two days, and he began to think that he was imagining things. At one stage he even thought he'd seen President Delman standing right across the street, watching him from afar. Crazy, he was going out of his mind inventing things.

Then it happened. Under cover of darkness, as these things usually occurred in The City. Only it wasn't Centuria, this time it was the President's guards. Same result, though, he still ended up in The Soak.

Jay wasn't even sure if he understood what the charge was. It seemed that he'd been blamed for the death of the nurse who'd sewn the WristCom into his arm six years beforehand. No evidence, of course, and he didn't even know who his accuser was.

Jay was removed to The Soak and less than a day after arriving there was rounded up with a group of inmates seeking justice in The Grid. He'd tried to protest that he didn't wish to seek justice there, he'd take his chances in The Soak, but a sharp electronic charge from the device wrapped around his neck knocked him to the ground. When he woke, the nightmare of The Grid had begun already – it was the first corpse to fall that roused him from unconsciousness.

The fight for survival had begun. Jay would do well in The Grid, years as a runner had made him healthy, fit and resilient. He'd worked with the inmates, keeping many of them alive for days and he'd won the hearts and minds of the viewing populace before the damning lies had started to turn public opinion.

Right up until the last moment, Jay had believed that he was going to make it, in spite of the horrible deaths of those he had tried to protect.

Jay Morgan was just another resident of The City to meet his end in The Grid.

When President Josh Delman watched Jay's last moments on the screen in his office, he breathed easy once again. Damien Hunter had been onto him, he'd traced events through the murder of the nurse. If Hunter got to Jay, he'd soon figure out where the evidence had been hidden.

Delman had used the BioPouch so that scanning equipment and security teams would never detect the device; it would be shielded as if it were a part of Jay's body from birth.

Although Delman had lost that particular piece of verification, he'd managed to elude Hunter once again. Hunter had his suspicions, he knew that the President was onto him, but without Jay he had no proof. The WristCom would die with Jay, it would go to the grinders and never surface again.

Jay was an innocent victim in all of this. He'd been chosen by Delman six years ago, almost on a whim. It could have been anybody, it just happened to be Jay. He was young and vulnerable, a quick check on the database and it was clear that he only had one parent, one who was wholly dependent on him. It would be easy to twist the knife, this kid would do anything he wanted and keep his mouth shut.

Delman's spies had seen Hunter's drive past, they knew that he'd put the pieces together and was closing in on Jay. If he got the WristCom, it would be a disaster. Jay had to go – and fast. The WristCom needed to go through the grinder, along with Jay, before Hunter worked out what had happened and cut it out of Jay's skin.

For Delman, Jay's demise was nothing personal. The death of his mother was just fallout from some necessary intimidation – again, it was nothing personal. Like so many deaths in The Climbs, there would be nobody to mourn or protest, Jay's life would be snuffed out and he'd soon be forgotten.

Only things hadn't played out the way that Delman or Hunter would have liked. Delman's evidence was now in the hands of a lowly tech-op, who hadn't yet realized the value of what he'd found among the bloody remains of Jay's body. Hunter knew he'd been beaten to it by Delman, and coupled with the appointment of Talya Slater he was enraged by the President's actions, anxious to steal this advantage from him as soon as possible.

Meanwhile, the device which both powerful men had sought had fallen into the hands of Max Penner, an operative who neither of them had ever even noticed. Penner had just taken the device from its hiding place and was looking it over at his desk. Just another insignificant worker, ten minutes away from meeting a new Law Lord who'd requested a tour of his facility.

Morning

It had been a long and uncomfortable night in the sewer. Joe and Lucy had managed to doze off occasionally, but the scurry of rats or the sheer discomfort of being perched so awkwardly in the pipe-way made unbroken rest impossible. Joe reckoned that if he could survive a night like that, his fear of the wretched creatures should subside. He just hated the things, they were a constant reminder of the squalor that he was forced to live in in The Climbs. It wasn't just him, there were millions packed into those decaying tower blocks while the privileged few led a life of luxury on Silk Road.

Knowing Lucy and Mitchell so well had helped not to make it an 'us and them' situation for Joe. It could easily have become that, but it reminded him always that most Silk Roaders were as trapped as he was. They were stuck in The City too and it made challenge and resistance impossible for all of them.

He and Lucy needed to step out after curfew. She wouldn't raise any alarm bells if she left The Climbs via a different exit, sometime after Segregation ended. She had to give it long enough to create the deception that she might have been in The Climbs from early morning, probably near 08:00 would be a good time to leave.

It was not uncommon to see Silk Roaders entering The Climbs on charitable missions. Talya was just one of many whose conscience did not permit her to switch off from what was going on in the tower blocks. There was nothing they could do to challenge city law or take on the establishment, but it still wasn't illegal to show some human compassion.

Wiz was back at the sewer entrance promptly at 06:00, he'd brought food and water. The three moved away from the pipe's outlet and found somewhere to sit and chat.

'How'd it go?' asked Wiz. 'You two stink, a bit of time in the open air will make the smell go away with any luck.'

Joe and Lucy had long stopped noticing it. For Lucy, it would entail a hot shower at home and a change of clothing.

For Joe, it would mean carrying the water that he needed for washing up more than fifty flights of stairs, then sponging himself down with ice-cold water. He'd then have to find his only other clothes, donated by Silk Roaders to a street store, and he'd have to do his best to handwash the old set in cold water.

Joe never felt as if his things were properly dry in winter, it was so difficult to get heat. It was crazy that he could access old tech on the black market, yet getting a bit of warmth into your tower-block apartment was almost impossible. He recalled his time on Silk Road as a child, but quickly dismissed the memories, it was pointless thinking about what had been, he needed to focus on the future.

They had ambitious plans in mind, and he knew how it might conclude. Lucy did too, they all understood that they were playing with fire. To even think of doing what they were doing was insane; they could all end up in The Grid, the next human fodder for the screens. The Grid was a constant warning about how dangerous this all was, but there seemed to be no other way.

Hannah was their safety net. If they ended up in The Grid, she could help them to survive, they'd have an ally on the inside. They'd kept her away from the sewer activity – if they ever got caught, Hannah needed to be well away from any suspicion. Only Lucy dealt with Hannah. Joe wasn't even sure if the two had exchanged full details of what was going on.

Lucy was anxious to hear from Hannah, having had no communications all night. She was unaware of the pace of events while she'd been cut off below ground. Hannah was already preparing for her first day at work with the Gridders. They were closer to the truth than they could possibly have imagined.

Joe and Lucy shared details of the night's breakthroughs with Wiz, making sure that the now accessible data from Matt's card was paired between devices. There were a lot of files in there. They'd need to go through them thoroughly, away from the sewer. That job would mainly fall to Lucy and Mitchell – Wiz and Joe had to rely only on solar charge, they were lucky enough to have device access at all. As Silk Roaders, Lucy and Mitchell could get to power supplies and the Fortrillium public mainframe, they'd be able to move a lot faster.

There was much speculation about the source of the second network. Having grown up in The City, none of the group could possibly imagine life outside the walls. In The Climbs, the majority of people had never even seen Silk Road, so they could only guess what it was like. Silk Roaders had access to The Climbs because that helped to focus their minds on what they had to lose if they didn't play nicely. But what was beyond Silk Road? The irony was, most Silk Roaders never asked, and they never dared investigate for fear of punishment.

The reality was that The City was made up of three concentric circles. At the heart was The Climbs, surrounding that was Silk Road, which had a well-defined perimeter. That perimeter was miles of rubble and wasteland, the remains of a fallen city. There was no life there, nothing to see, just several miles of decaying, levelled city. Beyond that, in the final circle, was a concrete wall, a hundred metres high, made from bricked-up and vacant tower blocks with the gaps filled in by a man-made barrier. No way out and no way in. It had to be that way after the plague years. The residents in The City believed they were the only ones left, it's what they were constantly told, The City was their refuge and sanctuary.

Within those concentric circles, a perfect equilibrium was maintained, with the poor stuck in the centre with no way out, and the affluent paralysed by their own complacency and comfort in the outer circle. At the heart of it all was Fortrillium, and Damien Hunter, and a President who seemed to be in charge – most of the time.

It was these institutions of power that the friends were taking on now. They'd already uncovered the first lie – perhaps the biggest deception. For all of their lives they'd believed that there was nothing beyond the outer walls, that life in The City was all that was left, all that was keeping them alive. But with the discovery of the second network, all of that was thrown into doubt. There was something else out there, something that wasn't Fortrillium. Everything in The City was Fortrillium – the thought that there was anything else in existence was almost unbelievable.

What was the source of that other network? Did it come from within The City walls or could there be life outside? Did Fortrillium – or the President – even know about it? If they did, why was it being kept a secret? They'd tried to explore the sewers over a year ago when their work had just begun. They were all dead ends, blocked by several levels of iron gratings, impossible to break through without power sources and heavy tools. None of those were options in The Climbs.

They all understood the dangers of pushing on further, but the thought of there being life outside the walls was tantalizing, it challenged the entire fabric of the society that had been built up inside the barricade. Were they the only plague survivors, as they'd believed for so many years, or was there more than this beyond The City's walls? They were going to find their answers within the next few days and the truth would be more astonishing than any of them could ever have imagined.

Hidden Assassins

Hannah was taken aback by the speed of it all. There was no standing on ceremony here, she'd been greeted and introduced, then it was straight down to work. She liked it that they referred to her by her Gridder ID – Janexx2 – that was respectful, and they were all clearly impressed by her performance in the competition.

She hadn't expected to get to make a start immediately, but they'd had a new intake that morning, and there was no better way to learn than on the job. Hannah wouldn't participate in the trial, but she'd get to create zones and present them for review. They'd assess her performance and give feedback to her. Depending on how fast she learned, she might get to construct a zone soon.

This was the closest Hannah had ever got to The Grid. She'd seen it on the screens, but there was only so much you could surmise from that. It was smart, the gamer in her loved it, but she knew not to become distracted; innocent people were being killed in these trials, they had to find a way to stop it.

On her console was the guide, the full rules for the trials that took place in The Grid. She read it quickly, feeling both amazed and horrified about what had been conceived.

The Grid was a huge hangar, the size of a small town. Its walls were flat, its ceiling domed. The perimeter, roof and floor were coloured blue, and close yellow lines ran along and across, creating a grid pattern throughout. This was an artificially rendered environment: anything that the Gridder team modelled on their consoles would be immediately generated in the arena. Entire environments could be created or destroyed in a moment, traps and hazards deployed, and food and water supplied – or denied. The Justice Seekers were at the whim of the Gridder whose job it was to do everything possible to stop them reaching The Core, the circular dome right at the centre of the hangar.

If they reached The Core, they got to walk away and make The Justice Walk. Not one person had ever made it to the centre before.

'This thing is amazing,' Hannah whispered to the Gridder seated behind her. 'No wonder nobody ever makes it out alive.'

'That's just it.' The Gridder's name was 97TRaider. 'If it were left to us, they would make it out of there.'

'What do you mean?' Hannah asked, intrigued by the answer she'd just received to an innocent question.

'Well, the Justice Seekers have been improving, they're getting harder to beat. We don't know if they've just seen the trials so many times on the screens or if something has changed, but we've had several recently who almost reached The Core.

'That guy Jay, for instance, he was minutes away, we thought we'd lost it. I'd have taken the rap for that, it was my zone. I'd glitched it, missed something obvious with all the pressure.'

'It's easily done,' Hannah offered, figuring that it would be best to make friends here rather than enemies. 'What happened?'

'I thought he was through and I was in big trouble, but I lost control of my console and something took over. The others swear it wasn't them, but it was like someone else finished the trial for me. It's occurred several times recently, whenever we get close to a Justice Walk someone takes over and completes the trial.'

Hannah didn't know what to say. 97TRaider saved her.

'There's someone else out there, you know, and it's very clear that they don't want anyone near that core.'

CHAPTER EIGHT

08:05 Law Lord

Talya was shaken. She'd known that things would get immediately challenging and tough when she became a Law Lord, but she hadn't expected the sudden turnaround that she'd just experienced. She'd barely had time to draw breath before she was being challenged and threatened by her fellow Law Lords. She'd been witness to a level of violence which – thank God – they weren't exposed to on Silk Road.

The easy course would have been to turn a blind eye, like everybody else who enjoyed the comfort away from The Climbs. But how could she? She'd been a victim herself. Who knows how she and Lucy had escaped the same fate as the Parsons family? It was as if someone was looking out for them. No, she'd been given a small break, it was her moral duty to do something about it, to do what she could to help.

They were living in a screwed-up world, that was for sure, but Talya still believed that it was possible to influence events. To do so, she'd have to live her life on a knife edge, challenging things wherever there was a glimpse of light, choosing her battles carefully and edging forward with the hope of lasting change.

She'd need allies too. She understood that the other Law Lords were terrified, it's always easier to bow to intimidation and pretend that nothing is happening. They were all complicit in the horrors of The Grid. Every time the citizens gathered around the screen to watch the fates of the latest Justice Seekers, they were making it more impregnable, they were forging the chains which kept them constrained.

They shouted at the screens, willing some of the Justice Seekers to success. They cursed and scorned the killers, thieves and murderers when they perished, and pretended all the time that this was justice and not butchery.

'An eye for an eye, a tooth for a tooth, a life for a death.' That was the slogan for The Grid, where justice was seen to be done. The viewers were little more than baying crowds, applauding the deaths. It didn't matter who was seeking justice in The Grid, no-one ever made it out alive, everybody knew that there was no justice, in spite of the charade they all took part in.

Talya understood that change came from bold and brave moves. She was petrified that she would be the one to upset the equilibrium, but it had to be done. By her. Lucy was fatherless because of this so-called justice system; they both knew that he'd been murdered, but what could they do to challenge Fortrillium?

Talya had bided her time. She'd been strategic, moving up the ranks, increasing her sphere of influence. She was at the top of the tree now, hanging on for dear life, but finally in a position where she could do something. That began right now, as she shook the hand of Max Penner, the man who helped to keep The Grid running smoothly.

This was the facilities tour that Talya had requested, the one which had been reluctantly and hastily organized by Damien Hunter. Damien wasn't present, he'd been called off to attend to some important business in The Climbs, and he'd informed the Law Lords that they'd be required for a second sitting later that afternoon. Talya felt the ominousness of his comments; he was using this technique as part of the constant intimidation that she now expected.

Max was surrounded by Centuria, there was no chance that he was going to be able to speak freely during this encounter. He was introduced as an 'operative' and he explained to Talya – uneasily she thought – how he ensured the smooth operation of the machinery in that area. There was no mention of the flesh grinders or the bots which were dispatched to clear up the human debris after each trial; all hints of anything unsightly had been removed.

Talya knew she was being conned. She had to play along. She could see how the Chief Centuria would move towards Max whenever it appeared that he was about to give an answer that was little too detailed.

By the time she'd finished talking to Max, Talya felt that she was no better off. Sure, she'd seen the facility which housed The Grid, but what had she actually seen? She was not permitted to enter the hangar for 'security reasons', even Damien Hunter was not allowed in there, all operations within The Grid were automated or serviced by bots.

Talya felt that Max was a decent man, and she'd like to have talked to him in a different environment, one that was a little more conducive to sharing information. However,

Talya got what she came for, even though nobody even knew it at the time.

She was leaning on Max's desk, asking him more questions which he would never be able to answer, when she caught sight of a circular object clumsily concealed underneath some paperwork. Max apparently hadn't been expecting a visit at such short notice, it seemed as if he'd been trying to hide something.

Generally, Talya wouldn't have thought anything of a WristCom in an environment like this, she assumed that Max might need one as part of his work. This one was different, though, she could just make out the letters etched on the back panel. They read 'TS' ... Tom Slater, her husband, who'd disappeared so mysteriously six years ago.

Talya was sharp enough not to mention it there and then, not with the Centuria in such close proximity. But sure as hell she was coming back to speak to Max later and next time she wouldn't accept anything but the truth from him.

08:17 Detained

Developments came fast on that morning. A casual observer might have commented that it couldn't have been random, somebody must have been orchestrating events. Zach Fuller was the first casualty. He was on edge, it had been a horrible night. Wiz had brought him supplies in Joe's absence; they'd come late, and he was already jittery, wondering what had delayed Joe. He hated being so dependent but what could he do? That damned leg, it made moving around the tower block impossible.

After Wiz had gone, Zach continued thinking he heard sounds out in the hallway. The broken door had made him extremely vulnerable – there was lots of evil lurking within The Climbs after dark and Zach was an easy target.

He retained the knife by his side. Good old Joe, at least he wasn't left entirely defenceless. With one hand on the weapon's handle, Zach drifted in and out of sleep. Nobody in The Climbs slept well – if it wasn't rats or thieves, then it was violent rows or screaming children. Many were in pain from illnesses which would never be treated by drugs, unless they could be obtained on the black market or via the charitable work of a Silk Roader.

Zach got the sense that something was going on outside in the hallway. There seemed to be a lot of hushed movements out there. He knew better than to go investigating in the middle of the night. There was no light in the tower blocks after dark unless people lit fires or had access to solar-charged equipment. Zach had neither.

It wasn't until sunrise had removed the fear of darkness that it happened. Zach had finally managed to doze off, the arrival of dawn had given him the confidence to do so. It was sudden and violent when it came.

Four Centuria burst into the apartment. There was no warning, Zach heard nothing beforehand, they just came out of nowhere, brandishing weapons as if he were some deadly threat.

His hand tightened on the knife. He was ready to use it but thought better of it. He was one, they were many, it was not likely to end well for him. Instead, he tucked it under what passed as a mattress – it might come in handy later. He didn't know why they were paying him a visit yet, it might be just an enquiry. Slim chance of that – if it was Centuria, you were usually in bother.

'Zachery Fuller, you are to be detained on the authority

of Fortrillium, as deliverers of justice, for the crimes of violence and withholding forbidden literature.'

Zach was about to protest, but he realized that he must have been snitched on by somebody – who would do that? They knew exactly where to search. Two Centuria went behind the remains of Zach's kitchen cupboards. They removed a false panel and took out nine damp, stained books, three without covers where they'd fallen apart from overuse. Another Centuria hauled Zach onto his remaining leg and retrieved the knife from under the mattress. All of the items were scanned – as evidence no doubt – and bagged up, and the Chief Centuria indicated to Zach that he should move.

'How am I going to do that?' he asked, but they were not in the mood for empathy.

'Walk or we kick you down!' barked the Chief Centuria, at least presenting Zach with some battered old crutches. They must have realized that they were either carrying him down or he'd need some sort of assistance. He could have done with the crutches after he'd lost his leg, he'd had to make do with lashed up poles for years. They were useless, but allowed him to get around the apartment at least.

Last time Zach had come up those stairs it had been on a makeshift stretcher after his accident. The severed stump where his leg had once been was bleeding profusely and it was touch and go as to whether he would even survive. Thanks to the efforts of the people in his tower block, and some drugs smuggled over from Silk Road, Zach did get through it but became a prisoner in his own home.

He placed the crutches under his armpits and began to make his way across the room, stumbling at first. The Chief Centuria slammed the butt of his weapon into Zach's back.

He stifled his scream, refusing to cower in the face of these bullies.

Step by step Zach made his way down the stairs of his block – there were fifty levels to tackle in all – it was laborious and painful. At floor ten, the Chief Centuria had had enough. He kicked away Zach's crutches and pushed him down the concrete stairs. Zach was booted down the remaining flights of steps. By the time he was thrown into the waiting van on the street outside, he was bloodied and bruised.

It was only going to get worse for him after that. They were taking him directly to The Soak.

08:23 Rules of Engagement

There was a buzz in the room; a new group was about to enter The Grid. The trial would not begin until evening when there were more people to watch on the screens. Fortrillium wouldn't want to waste an opportunity for striking even more fear into the citizens of The City.

97TRaider explained to Hannah how Fortrillium would create profiles of the Justice Seekers so that they'd be able to dramatize things on the screens. The Gridders would get digital access too – they were putting on a show after all. The Justice Seekers would get a hot shower. Usually it was the first they'd ever experienced if they'd been raised in The Climbs. They'd be patched up and re-clothed to make them fit for the viewing audience.

The Modes would then be determined. That's where the Gridders came in, they'd have to respond quickly to Mode choices and create and render the gameplay incredibly fast. Such was the pressure that most Gridders saw it as a personal challenge rather than murder. They never saw the live screen feeds, they were forbidden to watch in their role, they only saw the digital simulations on their screens.

Over the years it had been discovered that this was the best way to manage the Gridders. If they could think of what they were doing as gameplay rather than murder, it helped focus their minds considerably. The watching audiences saw and heard every last moment of a Justice Seeker's death. For the Gridders it was just another digital casualty. They were separated from the real human being who'd just lost their life.

'How do the Modes work?' asked Hannah. She'd seen the trials on the screens but never realized that there was an element of chance involved.

'They get a maximum of ten Modes,' 97TRaider began. 'It's completely random, nobody knows how it will play out. The lowest number is two, the maximum ten. Each Mode presents a different, deadly challenge, created by a Gridder who's allocated at random. The Grid itself is a vast, artificially rendered environment. We can make it appear however we want to – when they're in there it's real to them, even though it's recreated directly from the consoles in this room.'

97TRaider paused a moment, unsure whether to ask Hannah the question that he wanted to ask.

'Have you signed yet?' He dropped his voice. 'You know there's a catch to being here, don't you?'

Hannah felt a churn in her stomach. This was new to her.

'What do you mean?' she asked, not particularly wanting to hear the answer.

'You have to sign a second document, it's how they keep us on our game. If we let anyone through The Grid, they throw us in there to join the next batch.'

Like Talya, Hannah had known that she was exposing herself to danger. She'd imagined that she could walk away, that she could get the information they were after then turn her back on this job. She was wrong. This appeared to be a one-way trip.

'Is there any way out of this commitment?' she asked, beginning to panic.

'There are two ways to get out,' 97TRaider began. 'The bad way, which I just told you, or the good way.'

'And that is?'

'You make a hundred kills, that's the only other way out,' came the reply. 'I'm up to thirty-nine, just over sixty to go.'

This was not what Hannah had been expecting. This information was top secret, she'd already signed the document which would confirm her silence, and that's why none of this was common knowledge.

There was worse news to come. One of the Gridders had been in an accident overnight – and they were a Gridder down. City law decreed that there had to be at least ten Gridders to make all of the Modes available, there was nothing else for it.

It was an unprecedented move, but it was fortuitous that Hannah had arrived that morning. It was almost as if that accident had been arranged for the now deceased Gridder. The Head Gridder handed Hannah a console on which was displayed the document that 97TRaider had just spoken about.

'You'll need to sign this,' said the Head Gridder, handing it over.

'You're going to get a baptism of fire, you're going into the draw with all the other Gridders, you may even get some gameplay today!'

08:42 Alone

Harry had been expecting Lucy that morning, Talya had promised that she'd send her in her absence. Unknown to Harry, Talya and Lucy hadn't even had a chance to speak, events were moving so fast.

Harry wasn't sure what to do. Talya was her only link to the outside world – she needed water, it was hot in the apartment during the daytime, she'd need to drink.

08:00 or thereabouts Talya had promised, it was long past that now, Lucy must have forgotten. Harry glanced out of her window. The sun was going to be fierce, the glare would burn through what was left of her windows all day. She'd be baked in an oven. Harry smiled as she remembered cooking at home with her mum, in the days before the plague. She'd been tiny then, loving every minute that she spent with her mother, precious moments. If only they'd all known how cherished those memories would be. The epidemic had caught them all by surprise, nobody even saw it coming.

It was all inconsequential now, the plague had happened, wiping millions off the face of the Earth. For all she knew they were the only ones left, that's what Fortrillium told them. Harry thought otherwise. Even though she was so young when it occurred, she'd travelled the world even then. It was a big place, surely there must be others?

She'd learned a long time ago to keep thoughts like these to herself. Fortrillium was clear about that in its threatening public information films – there was to be no talk of the world as it was. Harry had lived through five generations in The City. She'd watched as Fortrillium's version of events had eroded the real truth until it just became accepted as how things were.

Harry was thirsty, she didn't have enough water to last the day. She'd need to pace herself in case Lucy didn't come. She reckoned that if she started to walk down the stairs she'd be able to make it there and back before nightfall. She could take her time, it would be safe enough. What choice did she have?

She wouldn't be able to carry much, she'd drink at the water barrel and take some back with her.

Harry closed the door of her apartment behind her, it had long ago ceased to lock properly. She began to shuffle along the hallway towards the concrete stairs. It had been a long time since she'd done this, but she was sure she could still manage if she took her time. Harry cursed her arthritis, it was so difficult to grasp the railing tightly. Her foot hovered above the first step, and she listened again to see if she could hear Lucy making her way up, but it was all quiet, not a sound up or down the stairwell. The workers left at 06:00, immediately after Segregation. If luck was on her side she might even catch one of the runners. Did they have any on her block? She wasn't even sure.

Harry began her slow descent of the stairs. Her legs were stiff, little used in her cramped living space so high above the ground. One ... two ... three ... Harry counted each one. She was doing it, she was sure that she could make it. Four ... five ... six ... She was getting faster, her calves burned with the effort but it was working, she was okay.

If she'd been able to continue like that, Harry might have made it. However, three floors below a door slammed as somebody left their apartment in a hurry. She heard them running down the stairwell at high speed and longed for a moment to recapture those days when she too would have had no trouble with that staircase. The noise from the slam startled a pigeon which had found its own sanctuary in an old light-fitting on one of the landings. It fluttered its wings in a bid to escape the perceived threat, flying up the stair-well and brushing Harry's cheek as it passed.

She knew that she shouldn't have reacted the moment that she flinched and lifted her hand from the rail. Her hand moved before her brain could stop it. She was in mid-step, the fall was inevitable. Harry reached out her hand, trying desperately to clasp onto the rail, but her arthritis – damn that arthritis – her hand was too stiff to steady herself. She'd put off taking Talya's pills that morning because she wanted to wash them down with water, they had a foul taste.

Harry appeared to be hovering in mid-air for a moment; she desperately tried to catch a hold of something – anything – to break her fall. As her frail, elderly body fell hard onto the concrete steps, she was conscious long enough to hear the snap of her arm as it broke clean through. She began to cry out in pain, but her head slammed on the unforgiving step, knocking her unconscious immediately.

With her body now relaxed and in motion, she rolled down several more steps before finally coming to rest at the bottom of the next landing, her head once more striking the hard floor. There was nobody making their way up or down the stairs, all was quiet. Harry's limp body rested awkwardly on the concrete. If anybody had heard her cry, nobody came to investigate it. You were best minding your own business in The Climbs, it wasn't wise to go in search of trouble.

As Harry lay motionless on the floor, a pool of blood began to form around her head. She was lifeless, completely still. Nobody would ever get to hear her stories of how the world had been before the outbreak, the memories would die with her. Nobody would ever know that her real name was Harriet and that she had once suffered several broken ribs when only a young child. They would never hear about the things that she had seen and done, and why the plague had come in the first place.

As the pool of blood by Harry's head spread out across the floor, the pigeon flew down and came to rest on her shoulder. It was the only living creature which knew she was there.

08:59 Captured

Lucy had spent long enough in The Climbs not to attract any attention heading back through the gate. Typically she used the exit closest to her home, but on that morning she felt it more prudent to pass Centuria who were not so familiar with her, to avoid a challenge. Her clothes had had plenty of time to dry out from being immersed in the water in the sewer, so although she was a bit smelly, she expected to go through without any problems.

She was anxious to catch up with her mum, who'd left several text messages on her WristCom. There was also a video message there from Hannah, but she dare not retrieve any of them, her remaining charge was hanging on by a thread. It helped to be out in the light again, where the device could recharge, but she didn't want to risk any kind of alerts when she passed through security.

She'd picked up Mitchell's early morning message confirming that she was clear of that day's roll call checks. She was safe to pass to the other side, they'd cheated the machines – this time.

Lucy was anxious to get back to her data. She'd made sure that Mitchell had a copy, which she passed to him over the network via secure encryption. That particular information needed to stay safe. If it fell into the wrong hands, they'd all be in trouble.

Joe was beginning to think about making a start with his runner duties. Their morning routines were all awry. Wiz had assured him that he'd got the message back to his mum that he was safe, but Joe was still anxious to get back to Jena and check in on her. She had become nervous and scared since his father's death, and who could blame her? His brother was still too young to take a proper role in fending for the family, he didn't share Joe's resilience. However reluctant Joe was to admit it, they were dependent on him. If anything ever happened to him, he feared the worst for them. And Zach too – there were many people who relied on Joe being there for them.

Lucy always walked up the security gates alone. It would not have been clever to tip off the Centuria that she had relationships in The Climbs. Many people crossed over to do charitable work or to provide practical support. Had Joe or Wiz approached with her, the alert sirens would have sounded, their own security chips never allowing them to cross over onto Silk Road. In fact, any attempt to try to make it over to Silk Road without authorization would have resulted in certain death.

The friends bade each other goodbye and headed off in their separate directions. However much they wanted to hack back into Fortrillium's network again, they had to give it a break for a few days, the last thing they wanted to do was to attract unwanted attention.

It was too late for that. Damien Hunter had had Lucy in his sights for several weeks, ever since President Delman had made the first unwelcome suggestion that Talya should become his replacement Law Lord. Hunter had fought and argued over that one, but he was blocked by the President. So Damien found another way around the problem.

To control Talya, he would need to hit her where it hurt most. She would withstand threats to her own safety, but no parent could ever cope with the direct intimidation of their child. So he started having her monitored and getting a feel for her movements and relationships. It didn't take long until he got involved personally. Lucy Slater was potentially of more interest than her mother. Whatever she was up to with those friends of hers could possibly lead him back to the information that had just escaped him. He'd been onto the man Jay, but somehow Delman had got a step ahead of him and made sure that Jay ended up dead in The Grid.

If Damien could stifle Talya, he could get to the President. If he could get his hands on Lucy, he would generate considerable leverage.

He couldn't have hoped for more. Lucy was involved in some surreptitious activity which amounted to treason. But even more than that it appeared that she'd come across information that would be useful to him, so he let the secret operation run a little longer, intrigued by what might be unearthed.

Every moment that Lucy and Joe had spent in the sewer the night before had been monitored by Damien and one of his best tech guys. They had recorded every bit of information, hopefully it would provide useful information about the President. Damien was forty years his junior, but he knew the stories about Delman's arrival in The City, and how he was the only known person to survive The Grid. Now Damien had got a glimpse into why that might be, why there seemed to be no records of the President in Fortrillium's database, just the legal documents confirming his right to his position.

Damien Hunter had what he needed. There was something beyond Fortrillium, a force that even he was not aware of. And he knew that it would lead back to the President. What Lucy and Joe had stumbled upon would likely be exactly what he required to hasten Delman's downfall. Without Delman, The City would be his, the firm grasp of Fortrillium would tighten immediately once Delman was gone. The President's deadly hold over him could be broken at long last.

So now he was done with the teenagers. Just as Lucy approached the gates, Damien drove through in his black car. He signaled to the Centuria who were on guard, and they grabbed Lucy's arms before she even realized what was going on. Her tech was taken away from her, she was injected with something that immediately made her unconscious, then thrown into the back of the windowless black van which was following behind Damien's car.

Further along the road, well away from the commotion at the gate, Joe separated from Wiz and arranged to meet up briefly with him towards the end of that day. Wiz wasn't sure what made him hang back and check Joe as he walked off in the distance. He'd just got a strange sensation that all was not well. Sure enough, just a few minutes after they'd parted, two vehicles pulled up alongside Joe. Wiz ducked in behind a wall, watching what was happening. Joe was wrestled to the ground, his tech removed from his bag, and then he was injected with something which knocked him out immediately. Two of the Centuria threw him contemptuously into the back of the van. Wiz saw enough to glimpse Lucy in there too.

He'd seen all he needed to see. He knew exactly what this was, it had happened so many times in The Climbs. His friends were being taken; he would have to go into hiding in case they were on to him as well. He'd need to tip off Mitchell and Hannah, but he didn't know how he was going to do that as he couldn't get over to Silk Road. He'd have to figure it out. Quickly. Wiz glimpsed Damien's face through the windscreen as the vehicles drove away. He knew then that his friends' lives were at risk. This was no routine questioning, they'd been rumbled.

Wiz would need to think fast. They were committed now, he'd need to steer this quickly to its conclusion. Whatever the result.

By 09:43 Lucy and Joe had been processed for detention, their limp bodies thrown into one of the cages in The Soak. Damien was ready to make his move. The Law Lords had been summoned to meet that afternoon. Talya Slater would be forced to preside over her own daughter's sentencing. Joe and Lucy were guilty of treason, they'd go straight to The Grid with the next batch of Justice Seekers.

He'd finish Talya Slater by killing her daughter and when Slater was gone he'd take down the President. Damien Hunter smiled to himself. Soon Fortrillium would have control of the entire city. Then he would begin his plans to reclaim his family and conquer whatever was beyond the walls.

CHAPTER NINE

Caged

It was the smell that Joe noticed first. For a moment he thought he was back in the sewer, but this was worse. It was the smell of humans, unwashed humans.

He forced his eyes open, it was a real effort. His focus was out at first, but soon it sharpened. He was looking at the bars of a cell, the realization made him sit up. He winced with pain, he'd been thrown into the vehicle with some force earlier, he was bruised and sore. Joe closed his eyes once again, wrestling with the pressing desire to sleep.

He had to stay alert. What had happened? It had been fast, he'd been aware that Lucy was in trouble, then they came for him. They'd got his tech. If they didn't know already they'd soon discover what he and his friends were up to. It was over, they'd been caught red-handed. This must be the place called The Soak. Joe forced his eyes open once again, lifting his head up from the floor of the cage. This time he focused beyond the bars in front of him and took in the scale of the place. It was massive, a vast concrete circular prison surrounded by multiple levels of cages lining the walls. Each cell was packed with human beings. In the centre, a tall, round watchtower manned by Centuria.

There was no comfort here. It was damp, cool and inhospitable. Joe could see a dead rat caught between the grilles of the cage below. Damn rats, was anywhere in The City clear of them?

He sat up and surveyed the area. Lucy was on the floor next to him, still out cold but beginning to stir slightly. There were six other people in the enclosure, four men and two women. Without warning, there was a crashing noise above them and everybody else in the cage dived to the ground. One of the healthier looking men positioned himself by Joe. He had a bad head wound, it looked like he'd had a run-in with somebody. The sound from the upper levels seemed to be getting nearer. Joe was aware of a sudden massive movement around the entire perimeter of The Soak.

'I'm Clay!' shouted the man. The sound was becoming deafening now. 'Lie down flat, put your hands on the back of your head, take a deep breath and wait until it passes.'

Water began to crash through the bars. It came with a crushing force, Joe was pinned to the floor. The noise was almost unbearable, like violent waves in a heavy storm. It never seemed to end, though it can't have lasted more than five minutes. Once the water had subsided, the bodies on the floor began to move again and Joe followed their lead.

'What was that?' he asked Clay, who offered Joe a hand to help him get up.

His legs were unsteady, he was appreciative of the assistance.

'Cleaning time in the cages,' Clay replied. 'It happens twice a day. Don't fight it, just get down and wait for it to pass. You'll be grateful for it in a few days, it helps keep the stink down.'

'I take it this is The Soak?'

'What gave that away?' Clay smiled.

The last thing Joe would expect in this place was humour. He was thankful that Clay had been the first person he spoke to. Joe checked on Lucy – the force of the water gush had begun to revive her, and she was trying to work out where she was. Joe went over to her, he figured she'd be grateful for a friendly face. He caught her up with events as she fought to regain control of her faculties. What-ever they'd been injected with had knocked them both out.

Lucy seemed quite calm about things considering what had happened. Living in The Climbs, the sort of people locked in the cages were familiar to Joe, but for Lucy this must have been a shock after life on Silk Road.

Clay brought them up to speed. They were in one of two holding cells packed with Justice Seekers who would shortly enter The Grid. Clay had already been in front of the Law Lords, but there was a second group – which included Joe and Lucy – who were scheduled for a session that afternoon. They'd got their neck devices fitted, Joe and Lucy too. They hadn't particularly noticed them so far, but when Clay pointed them out they began to feel tight and constricting.

'How did we get in here?' asked Lucy. She couldn't figure out the way in or out of The Soak.

'There is no way out,' said Clay. 'When they really want you, they'll come up on a hover pad and collect you, if not they'll make you use the ladders.

'Or we'll roll you out of the trap door if you die in here.'

Clay smiled when he said that, but it didn't help to put Joe's mind at rest.

'Here's a tip, by the way. When they do open the main door, always stand well away from it. When the doors open, you sometimes get a jumper. They always die, the cages are placed high enough above ground to make sure that nobody gets out crippled or with broken bones, they perish.

'Make sure you're out of the way when the door opens in case someone jumps, many people prefer it to rotting here or taking their chances in The Grid, it's quicker.'

Looking at the environment, Joe could understand why people would do this. It was already oppressive to him, he couldn't imagine what it was like after a week – a month or even a year. The days must have seemed endless, there was nothing for the detainees to do.

The sound of shouting and fighting broke out in the cage above.

'Get down!' Clay commanded. Lucy and Joe took his cue, he had become swiftly severe and urgent. Repeated gunfire sounded from the watchtower. The commotion stopped immediately and something red splashed onto the back of Lucy's shirt. It was part of someone's stomach – it had spread out through the grilles of the cages when the guns had found their target. Joe was grateful to Clay – he pulled the debris off Lucy and threw it to the back of the cage. A rat scuttled out and began devouring it. Joe wanted to scream, he needed to get out of this place, it was unbearable. No wonder so many opted for The Grid, it was the only chance of escape and release. Though it sounded like they had no choice, Clay said they were in that cage because they were already heading for trial.

Joe took a moment to run through his thoughts. He couldn't remember much about what had happened earlier, but Fortrillium must be onto them, they'd got his tech. What had they got to work with? Mitchell and Wiz weren't in the cages with them; if they'd managed to avoid detection, they would both be working to help them. Nobody had heard from Hannah, they'd been stuck in the pipeline all night, but Joe was hopeful that she'd made it through the Gridder Games. If she had, Hannah might also be able to help. They still had options, Lucy's mum would be able to exert some influence too.

They'd been onto something in the sewer. There was some level of intervention taking place at the end of the trials, from an external source. Could Mitchell and Wiz find a way to block it? Would Hannah be able to keep them alive long enough for them to figure it out? Too many questions. Joe needed to be able to speak to his friends, there was no chance of that in here.

'Stand away from the doors!' Clay alerted them. 'Someone is coming up.'

Joe heard an electronic whir at the front of the cell, then the door opened wide out into the void beyond them. There was movement in the cage. One of the men who'd been cowed in the corner stood up without warning. He was unkempt, bloody and starving, Joe could hardly believe that he had the energy to stand. He made a fast run at the gate, leaping out into nothingness, catching Lucy as he did so. She'd been slow to respond to Clay's alert and was caught off guard. As the inmate started his fall to the ground, gunfire began. If he wasn't dead from his injuries before he hit the floor, then he was after the thud onto concrete that followed five seconds afterwards.

Their most pressing problem was Lucy. She struggled to regain her balance and Joe thought for a moment that she was going to make it. Whatever they'd been drugged with earlier must have still been affecting her because she lost the battle and fell out of the front of the cage.

'Grab the side!' Clay shouted to her, rushing towards the open doorway. 'If she leaves the cell, they'll shoot at her!' Joe could sense movement in the watchtower as the Centuria gathered to take shots at Lucy. She was fair game if she left the cage without authorization.

Lucy's left hand had grasped at the bottom of the cage. It was all they could see of her and she just managed to catch the edge for long enough to give Clay time to dive to the ground. As Lucy's grasp was lost and she began to drop, Clay seized her wrist and started to pull her up.

'Help me!' he barked to Joe, whose reactions had been far too slow. The gunfire resumed, but they were toying with the inmates, the bullets did not find their target. Instead, they ricocheted all around them. Somebody got hit in the next cage. Joe heard the thud and the short cry of the woman who had been struck. She crashed to the floor, dead.

Joe rushed down to the mouth of the enclosure, narrowly missing a bullet. He called to Lucy to raise up her right arm. She was just hanging there, with Clay the only thing preventing her from dropping to her death. They must have been a hundred metres above the ground – Joe had enough time to see the crushed corpse of the man who'd jumped to his demise moments before. Still the bullets sounded around them, but they didn't seem to be trying to hit Lucy, intimidation appeared to be more their intention. Joe reached down and, working with Clay, they began to pull her up to the security of the cage. She was a dead weight, she had nothing to lever herself up with, she was totally reliant on Joe and Clay to haul her back to safety.

There was barely time to talk when they'd finally managed to get Lucy back into the safety of the cage. The Hover Pad levelled up with the doorway, coming to rest where seconds earlier Lucy had been fighting to stay alive.

As the Hover Pad met with the opening of the cell, four Centuria primed their weapons in case of any rush of attack from the inmates.

'To the ground!' one of them shouted, indicating with his weapon what he wanted them to do.

'Slater and Parsons step forward, raise your hands!'

The remaining prisoners crashed to the floor. Lucy and Joe turned to each other momentarily and then stepped forward. Lucy struggled to raise her arms above her head, it had felt like they were about to get torn out of their sockets when she'd been hanging from the cage. One of the Centuria placed his weapon to her head.

'Higher!' he shouted.

Lucy winced as she forced them upwards.

From behind the Centuria, Damien Hunter stepped out.

'Welcome to Security Facility Three,' he smiled. 'Though you may know it as The Soak.'

It all became clear to Joe. Hunter was going to finish them off. This wasn't a random arrest, they'd been targeted. Lucy and Joe kept their mouths shut, they were astute enough to realize that they weren't having a discussion, this conversation was strictly one-way.

'You are charged with treason and as such you will be moved directly to trial in The Grid.

'Thank you for all the fantastic research that you did on my behalf, it's going to be most fascinating working through the data on your consoles. You've saved me a lot of time and energy.

'If it wasn't for your damn mother, Lucy, this would not have been necessary, we might have been able to work together. I need to force Talya into a cage of her own, even if I'm going to struggle to get her in there.'

He drew something out of his pocket and walked towards Joe.

'You two will make a magnificent spectacle on the screens, I can't wait to see how things work out for you in The Grid.'

He injected Joe for the second time that day. This time Joe did not drop. Instead, he stumbled and was supported by one of the Centuria.

'You are a valuable prize, Lucy,' he continued. One of the Centuria moved to restrain her as she'd begun to take a defensive stance when Joe was injected.

'You're going to help me to hurt your mother. By the time we're done with you, she'll be as pliable as the rest of them. Even though she's going to try and put up a decent fight.

'They always try to fight, but they never win ....' were the last words that Lucy heard as he injected her with the sedative.

First Sight

Max was unsettled by Talya's tour. He couldn't remember the last time somebody had paid him a visit to ask him about his work. He'd been running the bots for seven years, his most frequent visitor was Damien Hunter who would sniff around like a hunting dog seeking new prey.

He was subject to routine security inspections by the Centuria – that went with the job, but nobody from outside Fortrillium showed any interest. They found the slaughter-house that he worked in abhorrent and chose to avoid it. The Justice Trials were public executions. However, they were presented to make them appear like genuine struggles for freedom. There would be massive excitement at times when it seemed as if somebody was going to make it through with their life, and the viewing figures rocketed. But it was their own fates that they were watching play out on the screens, the trials were there to remind The City that any attempt at resistance was ultimately futile. If they tried it, they would be exterminated. Not in a quick humane way, but slowly and publicly, so that everybody got to savour the moment when hope was crushed.

Max had long ago resigned himself to the situation. He'd been given the chance to escape from his miserable life in The Climbs. An aptitude for mechanics and tech had allowed him to raise his position from a lowly factory worker to someone with status and responsibility. He was far from being one of the affluent residents in Silk Road, in fact, he had no wealth at all other than the essential necessities in life. A roof over his head, food in his belly, protection from the cold and a few simple belongings. He knew what the alternative was, he'd spent twenty-seven years of his life in The Climbs and seen his sister, mother and father perish there. Max was a survivor, they'd be proud of him if they knew that he'd made it to the other side, he was alive, healthy and he had a good job.

Now things had changed. Max would not be human if he'd never wondered what went on in The Grid. He'd seen it on the screens but nobody ever went in there unless they were caught up in The Justice Trials. Not even Damien Hunter, though Max could tell he was desperate to be able to see inside. There was simply no way in or out, without having to take part in a trial; the bots were the only objects pre-programmed to enter – anything living that tried to get in immediately triggered the default trial settings, and that meant certain death for most people. Justice Seekers were different, they entered The Grid with a new implant, which disabled the default settings and enabled gameplay by the Gridders. If they survived their trial, the implants would allow them to exit via The Justice Walk, a hidden egress somewhere in the massive hangar which housed The Grid.

If Max hadn't found the WristCom while removing debris from Jay's body, he would never have thought of doing what he was about to do. But this could be achieved completely undetected. The knowledge would go no further, but he had to know. Now that the truth was within his grasp, Max wanted to see what was inside The Grid.

After Talya and the Centuria had left, he began preparing the maintenance bots for a sweep of the hangar so they could make sure it was ready for the new trial that would begin that night. They'd work in there for several hours, ensuring that the rendering grids were fully functional. They'd maintain the cameras which would display the action on the screens and make sure that the entrance was ready for the release of the Justice Seekers. Only this time Max was sending in an additional piece of equipment, the WristCom that he'd discovered, which had been secretly charging on his work area, concealed by a mass of paperwork.

He'd been careless. He thought for a moment that Talya Slater had seen the device, but he'd been quick to cover it, he was sure that it remained undetected. Max attached the WristCom to one of the bots, making certain that the video feed was displaying via a secure channel on his console. You didn't work with the bots for seven years and not pick up a few tricks that could come in handy every once in a while. Most of the time he used these skills to fix his stuff at home, but now he was using them for subterfuge, to make sure that what he was about to do would go undetected. It had taken him a short time to figure out the device. The feed was working well – Max would see everywhere that the bot went inside The Grid.

He released the maintenance bots into the long tunnel network which protected the hangar from entry by humans. To all intents and purposes it was a completely sealed area, the only living creatures which ever entered came out in the waste storage bags, ready for grinding, shredding, compacting and disposal. The bots made their way up the tunnel. Max watched his feed, riveted, prepared at any moment to close it down if anybody paid him an unexpected visit. Should be fine, a Centuria team would be there in a couple of hours to do the final pre-trial checks, but he was on his own, nobody would bother him.

He couldn't see much along the tunnels, they were unlit; the bots were programmed and they didn't need to see where they were going. Via the audio feed, he counted the five gates to reach The Grid. It took the bots twenty-one minutes to make it to their destination, and he reckoned, at the speed they travelled, it must be at least 7 km to The Grid. That took them beyond The City walls by his calculations; it would make sense if it couldn't be reached directly from inside the perimeter.

It took the WristCom camera a short time to adjust. His screen went white for a moment, but as the bot made its way through the final gate, there was light inside the hangar and Max had a full view. The Grid itself was vast, a huge empty area in what he thought was a domed structure – he couldn't get a broad enough view to be sure. There was nothing there, just a blue background with row upon row of criss-crossing rendering strips. This, no doubt, was why they called it The Grid, that's exactly what it looked like to Max, though people in The City never got to see it like that.

Max was frustrated – there seemed to be little to see.

The bots just made their fixes, checking the grid lines for damage or breakages, running a test on cameras, carrying out automated repairs where necessary. As they did so, items were updated on his maintenance inventory. Usually this was the only indication that the bots were executing their work; he never got a visual, that would have been forbidden knowledge.

Towards the end of the maintenance schedule, when Max's own inventory requirements were completed, something entirely unexpected happened. He'd been waiting for the bots to make their journey back down the tunnels, but they didn't, they began to move near the centre of the hangar. There were so many tram-lines in The Grid, it created an optical illusion, it was difficult to determine shape or structure there. To Max, it just appeared empty, but as the bots converged in the centre it became apparent that there was something else there, a construction of some kind. This was interesting information. As far as he knew, this delay at the end of the routine was due to the bots undergoing their own self-maintenance schedule. This part of the process was unknown to him and he didn't receive any data about it.

They seemed to be engaged in a repair task, but Max had no knowledge of this, it was not part of his own schedule. It appeared that he was not supposed to know about this. Did anybody else know, even Damien Hunter? How could they? The cameras within The Grid were only activated by the chips inside the Justice Seekers, there was no feed to the outside world until they entered the gameplay area.

Max didn't know what this was, but whatever its purpose the bots seemed intent on spending a lot of time there. Then there was movement, sudden and unannounced. A doorway opened right in front of the bots, then closed once again. Although Max saw it for only a moment, it was clearly an exit. Was this where The Justice Walk began? Was it true that you could get out of The Grid? He'd only caught a glimpse, but that was definitely an opening, right at the centre of The Grid. But where did it go? Max felt a leap of excitement, this was new knowledge; he wondered who knew about this, he'd never seen it on the feeds that they watched on the screens.

Then something happened – one of the bots seemed to falter as if there was some interference or technical issue. One of its arms began striking out haphazardly, hitting two of the bots to its immediate right. One of those bots was carrying the WristCom, and Max watched his feed as he saw it become dislodged and fall to the ground. The faulty bot went into auto-shutdown, but the damage was done, Max had lost the device. Damn, how could he have been so careless? He thought he'd secured it firmly – that must have been some impact from the faulty bot.

He cursed as his feed became a static view of the grid lines. He could only hear the bots now, there was nothing to see. They were retrieving the damaged bot for a return to the facility – it sounded as if they were heading back. The WristCom would lie there undetected during the next trial; the cleaner bots wouldn't go in there now until it was all over. When there would be new bodies to retrieve.

Max was angry. He'd got a glimpse of the truth only to have it snatched away from him before he could consider it properly. It seemed much clearer to him now. Whatever lay at the centre of The Grid was a secret, from him and everybody else who watched on the screens. There was an exit at the heart of The Grid – or was it an entrance? He couldn't be sure, but as he waited for the bots to return from their maintenance tasks, Max was certain of one thing at least. Whatever they thought they knew about The Grid had been wrong. There was a way out of that place, but nobody else had found it yet.

Condemned

Talya knew that her tour had been a complete charade, there was no way that Damien Hunter had allowed her to have any access to areas which he didn't want her to see. She'd seen Centuria training zones, Fortrillium server houses, and what was claimed to be the primary detention area for The City. What Talya should have seen was The Soak, but she was denied entry to that. Instead, her Centuria guide allowed her to see a video feed of what was supposed to be the main custody centre. Talya saw clean, well-fed detainees held in sanitary, uncrowded cells. She was not stupid – she knew that they were trying to throw her off the scent. There was no way that this was what actually happened to those found guilty of crimes in The City. Everybody had heard about The Soak, even if they'd never seen it. And she'd seen a group of detainees for herself already, their condition had been shocking.

Everything was a rush, no definite answers were given to her questions, she was denied direct access for 'safety protocol purposes'; everywhere she turned, Talya was blanked. They were hiding something, that was for sure, but would she ever get to the truth? Damien Hunter had orchestrated this deception. In fact, it was all so brazen there wasn't that much pretence about it. The message was clear: 'Don't push your luck, Slater!' This tour of the facility had been a direct defiance to Talya. Either she accepted it and played along, having gone through the whole pretence of 'approving' the good work of Fortrillium, or she could challenge again. She was supposed to go away happy with what she'd just seen. If she'd wanted to please Damien Hunter, Talya would have used one of her appearances on the screens to explain how reassured she'd been about the excellent, humane and fair justice system within The City.

Talya wasn't wired that way. She knew that every time she pushed, her life would be in more danger, but she would keep on pushing Hunter until she got closer to the truth. And she was going to see that man Max Penner as soon as she could, he was the only non-Centuria access she'd had all morning.

It was time for her to head back to The Justice Halls. Hunter had been adamant that they reconvene for a second sitting of the Law Lords. Talya felt weary. How many Justice Seekers would she have to send to their deaths before she could change this system? She would keep protesting and blocking with procedural matters wherever she could, but she was outnumbered by the Law Lords six-to-one, she'd be shouted down every time.

Talya dressed up in her legal robes and made her way to The Justice Halls, taking her seat next to Leianna Richwald once again. Damien Hunter was there, exerting his right as Fortrillium head to sit in on these proceedings.

Talya would never forgive herself for what she did next. As the next batch of Justice Seekers shuffled into the room, she barely glanced at them, ashamed of what she was about to oversee. She found the neck devices particularly distasteful, one more sign of oppression and control. A woman in the group began to speak.

'We here present demand the right to pursue justice under the laws of our city. As outlined in the Law of Retribution, we hereby request the right to seek a trial in

The Grid, to be granted our freedom in The Justice Walk if our innocence is proven. Our collective crimes are treason, arson, robbery, kidnapping and fraud. Will you give us our right?'

'Granted!' shouted Leianna Richwald, in a replay of the earlier session. Did any of the Law Lords ever challenge?

There was something about one of the Justice Seekers that caught Talya's attention. It was the posture and way of moving – she couldn't see a face, but it was familiar somehow.

'I challenge!' she called out.

There was an audible sigh among the Law Lords. Damien Hunter was watching Talya intently for some reason, as if he was waiting for her to see something.

Then she saw it. Two of the Justice Seekers seemed drugged, they weren't alert, they were just going through the motions.

'Lucy?' she asked. 'Is that Lucy?'

Her daughter was bloodied and dirty, she didn't have her wits about her, she was distant and vague. And that was Joe Parsons with her. Damien Hunter's revenge was swift and absolute. What had he done?

Damien's eyes gave the game away; he'd seen that Talya had finally realized what was going on, he was actually smiling now.

'Challenge overruled!'

He jumped up and intervened.

'As Head of Fortrillium I present the evidence files for Lucy Slater and Joe Parsons, proving treason against The City. Justice may only be sought in The Grid, under our most basic constitution.'

With a sweep of his hands, Damien sent the information to the consoles of the other Law Lords. Much of the data was redacted for the purposes of city security, but Talya got the gist quickly enough. Lucy and Joe had been caught red-handed hacking into Fortrillium networks. She knew why straight away – they were trying to discover the truth about their fathers, just as she was. Only they'd gone about it the wrong way, they should have remained out of sight.

Talya knew that there was nothing she could do. A charge of treason and this supposed evidence was all Hunter needed to send Joe and Lucy to their deaths. Her challenge stood, but the Law Lords voted against her.

Leianna Richwald turned to Talya and said, 'I told you. He sees everything, this has cost you your daughter.

'Was it worth it, Talya?'

The sentence was passed.

'The inmates may invoke their right for group justice, in which the crimes of the many are subsumed by all, and The Justice Walk will be shared by those whose innocence is proved.'

The Justice Seekers were led away. Lucy and Joe seemed barely aware of what was happening, they'd perish fast in The Grid unless they could get their wits about them again. What had happened to make them this way? They didn't stand a chance in there.

The trial would not begin until the evening. Talya had about five hours to see what she could do to help out Lucy and Joe. She'd need to see Wiz and Mitchell, they'd know what Lucy and Joe had been up to. And that man – Max – he was sure as hell getting a home visit as soon as he'd finished his shift.

Talya understood what was happening now – this was going to be her final fight for the truth. This would either end in her death – and the death of her daughter – or she'd succeed in bringing down Damien Hunter and this entire corrupt system.

If Lucy perished in The Grid, Hunter was dying anyway. If Lucy died, she'd kill him with her own hands. She would be his judge, jury and executioner.

CHAPTER TEN

Fugitive

Mitchell had been quick to figure out something was wrong so he fabricated excuses at his workplace, making his way to The Climbs as soon as he could. There were no sick days for workers in The City's inner core, but as a resident of Silk Road Mitchell was blessed with a little flexibility. He'd been unable to raise Lucy via her WristCom after their early morning exchange. That made him panic straight away, particularly given what they'd just discovered in the sewer.

He headed for Joe's block first of all, running the fifty-two flights faster than he'd ever managed before. He rattled Joe's mother bursting in as he did, but he knew that there was no time to waste.

'Have you seen Joe today?' he asked. Jena said very little, nobody had heard her talk at any length for many years. It was Joe's brother who replied. They hadn't seen him since the day before, but Wiz had been around to let them know he was okay.

'But nothing from Joe this morning?' Mitchell asked again.

A shake of the head from Dillon.

'Okay, Dillon, you need to take Joe's runner duties today. Do what you can. I'll let you know when I've found Joe. He may be in trouble, I don't know yet.

'Dillon, you're in charge here, do you hear me?'

Dillon nodded. Mitchell wasn't sure he was up to the task, but if Joe was in danger they'd both starve if he didn't take a lead.

'I'll be back as soon as I can. Stay safe, Jena.'

Jena looked at him. He could see the fear in her eyes, she thought it was all happening again. She was terrified that she was going to lose her son just as she'd lost her husband six years previously.

Mitchell left them as swiftly as he'd arrived. He ran down the stairs cursing The Climbs for the lack of elevators. They'd never worked in his lifetime – those that weren't stuck between floors were used as living spaces. Anywhere which could keep a human being from dying outdoors in the cold.

Wiz didn't live too far away and, fortunately, his apartment was only eight levels up. Mitchell made it no further than the entrance to his block. Wiz had hidden outside, watching to see if the Centuria came for him. Wiz's parents had died a long time ago, he'd virtually raised himself in The Climbs; he and Joe had met each other through their black market connections.

'Hey, Mitch. Over here!' came the whisper.

Mitchell checked out the area. Wiz was hiding behind a pile of debris that had been abandoned on the street.

'What the hell is going on?' asked Mitchell, and Wiz filled him in as best he could.

'What are we going to do?' asked Wiz, interrupting the silence that had followed his update.

'I have the data and Joe's unlocked the files with genetic encryption already,' began Mitchell. 'We know there's a second network that intervenes at the end of the trials. That's if they even send Joe and Lucy to The Grid,' he added. But both of them knew city life well enough to know already that that is exactly what would be happening.

'We need to isolate and control that network. If we can do that we might be able to save them.'

'What about Hannah?' Wiz queried. 'Has anybody heard from her yet?'

'She got in, she won the Gridder Games, but I don't know if she'll get anywhere near the trials. She may be able to help us, though. We need everybody working on this.'

'Are they on to us though?' Wiz wondered. It was why he hadn't risked entering his apartment, in case they came for him.

'I got through the gates okay,' Mitchell offered. 'Hopefully they don't know about us yet. We need to set up in a secure area – can we hop the data from the pipeline to somewhere nearby?'

'If you can get me the tech, I can do the work. We'll need to go into the sewer from the second entrance. I know it's trickier but they're sure to have a camera on the main access point now.'

The public screen on Wiz's square burst into life. The Climbs was plagued by this at any time of day or night. If Fortrillium or President Delman wanted to say something, they had little care for whether people were sleeping or not. When they wished to make an announcement, they just did it, and it was extremely hard to avoid. Those in The Climbs who didn't have access to tech just had to tolerate the blasting audio from the outdoor screens positioned on every block.

This was good, though, a new Justice Trial was being announced, and they'd get to see who was going into The Grid that night. There was a repeat of the first batch – Clay's group – who'd already been announced. Then came Joe and Lucy and the other wretches who'd be forced to enter with them. Wiz and Mitchell just watched, unable to find the words to describe what was unfolding in front of them.

'Treason,' said Wiz, after the glossy video trailer had finished. 'And they're in with murderers, fraudsters and thieves. There's no choice for them – if they're pushing for treason, they'll go directly to The Grid.'

'Lucy's a real coup for Fortrillium,' it occurred to Mitchell. 'Damien Hunter will make Talya suffer for this. Did you hear they made her a Law Lord? I don't think Lucy even knows it yet, it's been on the news.'

The news was not something that people like Wiz got to keep up with much in The Climbs. Survival tended to be of more importance.

'Sorry,' said Mitchell, realizing his mistake. It was easy to forget what Joe and Wiz had to put up with – he thought of them as friends, they were just the same as him. Only, after Segregation every night they were different, they each had to retreat to their homes where they were always reminded who the real winners were.

Wiz's attention was caught by a black vehicle driving around the corner. He urged Mitchell to duck down. It was Centuria, they were coming for him. He couldn't be sure of that until they'd had time to reach the eighth floor where he lived.

They shot out the glass that still remained in his apartment windows, and then threw the few things that he owned out onto the ground below. There was no care taken as to whether there was anybody walking in the path of the falling debris. A small and battered wooden table crashed to the right of a mother and her child, forcing them to duck into the side of the tower block to try to take cover. Wiz almost went to help, but Mitchell held him back.

'They're okay,' he said. 'Stay back.'

The Centuria were in and out of his high-rise in minutes. No need for Wiz to see what they'd done to his apartment. He was homeless now, a fugitive.

He'd be able to hide in the dark corners of The Climbs, but the real problem would be if they were on to Mitchell. Without his access to Silk Road they were lost, they'd never manage what needed to be done to keep Joe and Lucy alive.

Honesty

It was all Talya could do not to rush at Damien Hunter and scratch out his eyes. He'd made his move now and the gloves were off. Joe and Lucy's trial would begin at 20:00, after Segregation; they never risked launching a new trial before they'd separated the residents of The Climbs and Silk Road. That gave Talya just under five hours to get battle-ready.

Lucy and Joe could be dead before the end of the night, though she suspected that Damien would make sure they stayed alive for long enough to bleed the political capital from the event. This was about Talya and Damien Hunter, it had little to do with Lucy and Joe.

Talya didn't give Hunter the satisfaction of a response. She kept her eyes on her drugged daughter until she had fully exited the room, then she rushed away, throwing up in the cubicles before she left the building.

She needed to find Mitchell and Wiz first of all. They hadn't been sentenced so she assumed her daughter's friends were safe – so far. She was going to make a house call on Max once his shift was over and push him about the WristCom. She was also going to risk a visit to Harry. It was dangerous for her going into The Climbs now she was a Law Lord, but she had no choice, this was her daughter's life. She wanted to know more about President Delman and what had happened when he walked away from The Grid.

She thought about Harry. Lucy would not have been able to visit her if she'd been apprehended that morning, and Harry might have been beginning to worry. First stop needed to be Harry, after sending a poll call to Mitchell via her WristCom.

As Talya entered The Climbs, she could tell that her arrival had raised eyebrows. Her pass data had been updated. She knew this is how it would work, each journey would now get flagged to Fortrillium. No doubt Damien Hunter would take an interest in all of it.

'Reason for your visit?' asked the Centuria guard.

No extra politeness now that she was a Law Lord.

'I need to make a charitable visit,' Talya began. 'Due to the detention of my daughter today I need to make alternative arrangements for a ward of care.'

She spat out the words about the arrest with barely repressed rage.

'This should be the last time I need to cross over,' she added.

Just the right combination of anger, resentment and honesty, she hoped. It was reasonable that she'd have some preparations to make after Lucy's arrest, but if she was too polite about it, it would not ring true. They scanned her through, and Talya was on her way. She'd need to make it brief, the last thing she wanted to do was to arouse suspicion.

She took a well-known route through The Climbs, heading directly for Harry's tower block. She cursed the stairs that she'd have to climb – you couldn't do anything quickly in this part of The City. Up and up she went, getting increasingly out of breath as she did so. She was beginning to lose count of the number of landings that she'd passed when she came to a pool of congealed and drying blood on the staircase. Talya stopped dead. She hardly dared to move on, this was a floor or two below Harry's, but she needed to investigate.

Talya walked up the stairs, there was a lot of blood. Further along, a body. There were rats there, not yet eating, but waiting like vultures to begin their feast. Talya instantly recognized that it was Harry, and she rushed over waving away the creatures from their intended feast.

Harry was bruised and bloody, she was like a small child curled up on the ground. Talya felt for signs of life – if the rats hadn't begun to eat, the chances were she was alive, a possible threat to the vermin waiting to devour her.

Talya cradled Harry in her arms, trying to detect a pulse or breathing. Her WristCom vibrated and she could see that Mitchell had picked up her poll. There was no standing on ceremony.

'Where are you? Do you know what's going on?'

'They've got Lucy and Joe, they're after Wiz, he has to stay hidden,' replied Mitchell, as anxious as Talya to share as much information as they had between them.

'They're going into The Grid tonight. What were you doing?'

Mitchell and Wiz glanced at each other. Normally this

would be between just them, but looking at Talya's face on the small screen, evasion was not a good tactic.

'We've deciphered Joe's data card, we've been trying to figure out what happened to Matt and Tom.'

Talya heard Wiz's voice off-screen. She cursed Lucy's curiosity – she had been so busy plotting her own revenge, she'd never even considered that Lucy and Joe might also want their own answers. They were as good as adults now, why shouldn't they want to get to the truth as well? She was angry, mostly out of frustration with herself, but she wished that Lucy had shared what she was doing, she might have been able to protect her better.

'There's something going on with the trials. We found another data source which isn't Fortrillium,' Mitchell picked up. 'We think someone else is finishing them off. Nobody is supposed to take The Justice Walk.'

'Can you save them?' Talya asked bluntly, she wasn't in the mood for conjecture.

'We need a safe house to work from, we've got to conceal Wiz and get a link-up to the data streams. If we can do that, I think we can help. They're going to have to keep themselves alive in there too, we can't do everything.'

Talya nodded at her WristCom – whatever they could do to help Joe and Lucy, they'd still have to achieve what they could on their own to survive. They had seemed to be in such bad shape the last time she'd seen them, she wasn't so sure about that.

'I need you both here at Progressive Block. Harry has had an accident, but she might be able to help us too. Can you get your hands on any med supplies, Wiz?'

Although she'd never been explicitly told so, Talya understood that Joe and Wiz would have black market connections – how else could they survive? She'd never met

Wiz, only heard Lucy talk about him, but if Lucy liked him she knew he'd be okay.

'I need bandages, painkillers and disinfectant. Can you get any of that?'

'I'll get them, don't worry. The dressings might not be new, but I think I can do it.'

'Do what you can, as fast as you can,' replied Talya. 'Wiz, you can hole up at Harry's and take care of her as well. Mitchell, you need to sort out the tech. Are they looking for you?'

'I don't think so. I wasn't at the sewer last night, they must only just have discovered what we were doing there. I think I'm safe, there's nothing in the equipment they have that will track back to me, they'll just see that Lucy and I are friends, no big deal in that.

'There's one more thing – have you heard about Hannah?' Mitchell added.

'She's joined the Gridder team, we thought we'd better get someone on the inside so that we had another route into Fortrillium.'

'Has anybody spoken to her yet?'

'Not yet, she can't be tracked back to what we've been doing in the sewer, we kept them separate. They'll only know about her relationship with Lucy, there's no way they can connect her with the treason charges.'

Talya wasn't so sure. She'd seen enough of Damien Hunter's work already to know that if he wanted to he'd be able to remove everybody in Lucy's circle of friends. And he was likely to do so too, just out of spite.

Harry started to gasp. It had helped her breathing when Talya laid her head on her lap. She seemed small and weak, Talya had to make sure Harry was okay.

'Let's move,' she said. 'Wiz, I need you here as soon as

possible. I have to get back to Silk Road. Mitchell, get the tech sorted out and make a start. The trial begins at 20.00. We need to give them whatever help we can.'

'What will you be able to do?' asked Wiz hopefully. 'Can you do anything as a Law Lord?'

'I'm as powerless as you,' came the reply. 'But I know a man who can help me. Get over here as soon as you can and I'm paying him a visit next.'

Watched

Reevil96 keyed into his terminal. This was different tech from the equipment used in Fortrillium, more advanced and much more to his liking. He proxied into Hannah's console, undetected, ready to watch her every move. He already had access to the other Gridders, he knew their gaming preferences, strategic techniques and play styles intimately. He'd watched Hannah's performance in the contest and was intrigued. She was different, her approach unique. As if it had been studied and learned, not developed over time.

She'd be a wild card in the next trial. It always took a while to get used to new recruits – you could never be sure which erratic move they might make next. She'd be easily beaten, though, they all were. They were given the scraps at the table, the illusion that they could control events in The Grid. But when the time came, he would make his play, just like he always had. It would be he who would deal with Lucy Slater and Joe Parsons as the entire city watched the spectacle on their screens. They'd get the surprise of their lives when the time of reckoning finally came.

CHAPTER ELEVEN

Psyched

Joe woke up feeling as if he was about to be sick. He was cold and uncomfortable, and for a moment he wasn't sure if he was at home. He wished he had been. As he focused on what was around him, it felt like a replay of earlier, when he'd come round in the cage. Clay's was the first face he saw. He was relieved about that, this man had already shown himself to be an ally. Opposite him was Lucy, struggling to come round from whatever sedative they'd been given.

He thought back to Damien Hunter's face, he wanted to kill that man. By nature Joe didn't have a violent bone in his body, but it was true, he wanted to kill him. Truth be told, he'd always wanted to kill him, ever since his father was taken from them. It was a hatred that had burned inside him, incubated by frustration and a sense of helplessness. As he'd changed from a boy to a young man, that bitterness had become focused on finding a solution – or information, anything to help him discover what had happened to his dad and Tom. But when he saw Hunter earlier, he realized that it was contempt that had driven him all along.

He hated that. So much of his life had been dominated by those events. He didn't think he was a spiteful person. In fact, he did everything he could to help not just his family but others in the same block who needed his help. But Joe wanted Damien Hunter dead. He didn't know how – or when – or if he would even be able to do it if the time ever came. Would he be able to show forgiveness if he managed to face his tormentor as an equal? Joe wasn't sure, he doubted that he could do it. Perhaps the anger was just a fantasy which had driven him to where he was now. Caged and defenceless. But the man had poisoned his life.

Clay smiled at him and helped him to his feet once again. There were other people in the room. It wasn't one of the cages, this was cleaner and more modern. They'd been re-clothed, dressed in brightly coloured overalls. He recognized these from the screens. Green overalls, the colour reserved for traitors. Clay was in blue, Lucy was in green, just like him. Traitors got a hard time in The Grid, they'd save something spectacular for them. If they stayed alive long enough. Joe knew what happened in The Grid, he understood that nobody ever made it out alive. So why wasn't he giving up? He still felt ready for the fight ahead. Of course, he was terrified, but he would fight and survive as long as he could. He would work with the others too, keep as many alive for as long as possible.

He wondered what it was about humans which gave them hope when all the evidence pointed to their sure and certain demise. He'd seen it on the screens – some Justice Seekers had given up before they even entered, they just wanted death to come as soon as possible. Usually it did. But the others were fighters, you could see it in their eyes. They were alert from the beginning, they were warriors. Joe knew what his chances were, and he chose to fight. It was always the fighters who made it to the end. The ones who worked together survived longest too. Clay would work with him, Lucy too. He'd get to know the others before it began, see who wanted to team up.

Lucy stirred, she'd been awake longer than Joe, but the sedative had hit her hard. She threw up on the floor, it sounded guttural and painful. Joe crouched by her, placing his hand on her shoulder. There was not much he could do to help, but at least she knew she wasn't on her own.

She recovered quickly, apologizing to everybody for the mess. Most of the inmates in the cell avoided her gaze, they weren't ready to commit, not sure if they'd be looking after themselves or teaming up with others. They were watching and waiting, deciding how things would play out.

It was more sanitary here than in the cages. Joe reckoned that was for the benefit of the screens – they needed them washed and clearly identifiable so that they could be easily picked out when the trial began. He hadn't been aware of the process taking place, but he'd had a soaking earlier, and he felt cleaner than he had for many years. Lucy had recovered herself and everybody had stepped away from the area where she'd vomited.

A guard came to the bars, not Centuria but Fortrillium still, and pressed a button to the side of the cell, out of reach of the prisoners. There was a sudden movement by Clay's feet. He jumped, assuming it was a rat. In fact, it was a small circular vacuum cleaner which scuttled across the floor, cleared up and disinfected Lucy's mess, then returned to a concealed area along the edge of the cell. There was a visible sigh of relief in the enclosure, the stink had been unpleasant. Usually in The Climbs the smell of the inhabitants was what dominated, but with all the detainees clean, it was Lucy who'd caused the problem.

'Psyche-Eval in ten!' yelled the guard, disappearing as quickly as she'd arrived. The inmates glanced at each other, some of those glances were becoming more friendly as a fundamental level of trust began to form among some of the inhabitants of this cramped area. Like animals sniffing for a scent, so the prisoners began to seek out alliances, tentatively at first.

Clay was first to speak. 'Anybody know what Psyche-Eval is?' he asked. They were all wondering, fearful of what might follow. They'd all seen the screens. Lots of data was presented about each Justice Seeker, particularly information about fears, vices, psychological problems and phobias. None of them had ever wondered where that intelligence came from, now they all suspected that they were about to find out. There were no answers to Clay's question, just shrugs, so he moved on.

'What's the deal with you two?' he asked, looking at Lucy and Joe. 'We don't see green overalls often in The Grid.' He sounded as if he'd worked there all his life, but they knew what he meant.

'Sticking our noses in where they weren't wanted,' Lucy said. 'Look where it got us!'

'A visit from the Head of Fortrillium, you must have annoyed someone!' he smiled back. Funny how humour seeps in everywhere, thought Joe, even this place of no hope.

'We got caught red-handed, we must have stirred up a hornet's nest, they were onto us immediately.'

Joe avoided mentioning Wiz, Mitchell or Hannah, he

didn't know if their conversations were being monitored. He thought it best to keep quiet about the details for the time being.

Clay decided to join in the confessional.

'I'm in for counterfeiting. We were getting people through to Silk Road for medical treatment.'

Joe and Lucy just stared at him.

'Really?'

'Yeah, I've been doing reconfigs on WristComs for years, took them this long to catch me. Never did it big scale, couldn't get access to enough devices, but we saved enough lives that way. A doctor on Silk Road helped us, but they only caught me – didn't find out how the units were being used, never suspected, I don't think.'

Joe and Lucy introduced themselves. If only they'd known Clay before they ended up in The Soak, they could have made good use of his talents. It hadn't occurred to them before, but there was probably a unique skill set among that group in the cell.

'Anybody else want to speak up? Might be a good idea to do it now.'

Clay surveyed the four other people, waiting for one to make a start.

'If we're going to survive in there, we need each other,' he continued. 'If you've got skills, tell us now.'

One of the women stood up, she'd been evasive up to this point. She was probably twenty years old, or close to it. Her face was hard, though, it was etched with the scars of a difficult life.

'Marjani,' she stepped forward. 'I'm here for murder.'

They knew that already from her red overalls. They hadn't judged – red overalls were considered marginally better than green. If you were wearing green, you were in for a hard time. Not from your fellow Justice Seekers, it was Fortrillium who were chasing you. They wanted you dead.

'Just call me Marjani,' she carried on. 'And it wasn't strictly murder.'

Everybody stared at her expectantly, waiting for her to continue.

'I broke the necks of two Centuria,' she said.

'Three of them killed my baby. Only two of them made it out alive and the third isn't safe until I take my final breath.'

Joe liked her immediately. The concept of crime in here was fluid. With anybody who knew how cruel the Centuria could be, that counted as revenge, not a criminal act.

Marjani's story gave another man courage to offer his own account. He was dressed in purple overalls.

'Miron Panko, arson.'

Brief, but everything they needed to know.

'Real arson or something else?' Clay asked.

'Depends on how you view it,' Miron smiled. 'We had a gang holed up in our block stealing food from families, ill and old people. I helped them build a fire to keep warm ... only I couldn't find any firewood, so I used them.'

Everybody chuckled at that one. Most people had been a victim of gangs at one time or another, those in The Climbs at least. It was good to hear of someone getting their revenge and evening things out.

The sturdy, bearded man who'd so far been silent in the corner stood up and neared the group.

'Ross Donaldson.' He held out his hand, the others were not sure what he was doing.

'Sorry,' he said. Handshaking was a custom used only

on Silk Road, it had died out many years ago in The Climbs. That gave the game away, few people living on Silk Road ever ended up in The Grid. Why would they, they had everything?

Everybody glared at him, he was not one of them. To Joe's shame even he became defensive. Silk Roaders who ended up in The Grid were usually psychologically ill: murderers, thieves and arsonists who couldn't help themselves. Not people who had to do these things to survive.

Ross sensed the unease. 'Assault!' he announced, by way of explanation. 'Though I prefer to think of it as feedback. I caught my supervisor embezzling money and had a quiet word with him that he ought to stop, in case someone else got to know – someone who'd inform on him. Instead of thanking me, he changed the paperwork trail so it looked like it was me.'

'Why do you call it feedback?' asked Clay.

'I snapped both his arms. That's my way of leaving a negative review.'

He chuckled at his own comment. It was infectious, the others laughed too. It broke the ice. Joe thought things were looking good, but this was only their cell. Up to fifteen people usually entered The Grid at one time, there were probably more.

There was one woman left, she was not willing to offer her name or take part in what was going on.

'You're welcome to join in at any time,' Clay offered. 'Whenever you're ready, just tell us, we'll help however we can.'

The mood in the cell was better, but a noise had started up to the side of them. It was a cross between wailing and shouting, somebody in one of the cells was highly distressed.

It bothered Joe – they couldn't see who it was, but they were isolated by the sound of it.

'It may be a patient from the Institute?' Lucy suggested.

Everybody knew about the Institute, but it was another of Fortrillium's dark secrets. People with mental health issues went there, for treatment or incarceration, nobody knew. What was clear was that in every trial there was usually somebody who had come from the Institute. Often they were first to die, unable to defend themselves or sometimes even understand what was going on. It was just one more sight that had enraged those watching the screens, as they saw lives being taken mercilessly before them. Joe's eyes moistened, he'd always been over-sensitive to the plight of others, he knew it made him vulnerable. He just couldn't hold back, he was a sucker for anybody in need. He called along the corridor to the guard.

'Hey! Somebody here needs help!'

No reply, no sound of movement, just the distressed sobbing of the person in the next cell, male or female, Joe couldn't tell.

'Hey! Can you help out here, please?'

He hadn't finished his sentence before the guard reappeared. She thrust an electrified mace straight through the bars, plunging it towards Joe's chest. She held it there as the shock from the charge stopped Joe dead in his tracks. He seemed paralysed, just shaking as the baton passed a massive voltage through his entire body.

'Get off him!' shouted Lucy, rushing to his defence, pushing the guard away through the bars. Clay had to pull Joe off the baton, it had clasped into his skin, that's what was keeping him there. A small patch of blood formed on his overalls as the hook tore through his skin, and he crashed to the ground, still shaking from the charge.

'I just found my first volunteer for Psyche-Eval,' said the guard as she hooked the baton into Lucy and began opening up the cell doors.

Spurned

It seemed to take Wiz forever to get back to Harry's apartment with the supplies. That was only because Talya was torn between taking care of her injured friend and putting the events in motion which she hoped would save her daughter's life. If only Jena had not been so cowed by what had happened. They'd both lost their husbands, but why hadn't Jena fought like her? They could have done so much more together. Talya needed allies and they were fast becoming fewer and fewer.

She had a couple of hours before the trial began. They'd always wait until the workday ended. The whole point of The Grid was to frighten, intimidate and suppress; it demanded the largest audience possible. Talya thought back to previous trials. The pattern was always the same. They'd soften up the Justice Seekers first, nothing to be gained in finishing it too fast. There would be a few shocks, perhaps a death or two, depending on the numbers seeking justice, but the early hours were played for dramatic purposes. They'd want Lucy to survive until the end, Joe too probably. If it followed the pattern, Lucy should be fine for several days, but she couldn't guarantee that. If Damien Hunter wanted her dead, she was sure that could be arranged.

Talya thought about Lucy and her near lifelong friend and wondered if they had what it would take to survive in The Grid. Lucy and Joe were sharp, smart, intelligent and resilient, they'd had to be, losing their fathers like that. But were they fit enough, strong enough – violent enough even?

The few Justice Seekers who made it to the end were powerful, athletic types, able to run, fight, jump and defend. Talya wasn't sure how Lucy and Joe would fare in that arena, but then she had been caught by surprise by what the five friends had already accomplished together. But they'd been caught, how had they got detected so quickly?

Talya stopped goading herself with the endless and terrifying possibilities. She would be as much use as Jena if she couldn't focus and figure out a way around the problem. Jena might be part of the solution here, she could at least care for Harry while Mitchell and Wiz were working with her to save Joe and Lucy. Talya resolved to concentrate on actions, not possibilities. She would need all the sharpness and strategy that her legal mind could muster in the hours ahead. And she might need to use a bit of violence herself – she was determined to make the most of her meeting with Max. The one that he didn't even know that she'd scheduled yet.

Talya picked up Harry from the stairwell – she was heavier than she'd expected – then returned to her apartment up the stairs. The bloody trail left by her fall was spattered across the steps, and Talya winced at how painful it must have been for her old friend. She placed Harry on what passed as her bed in The Climbs. As she surveyed the dirty pile of old blankets, rags and discarded clothes used to soften the hardness of the concrete floor, anger surged through her body. Harry made light of the conditions that she had to endure, but Talya's sense of human justice cursed that someone so elderly could not be cared for with more dignity and compassion.

Harry had known life before the plague, she was one of only a handful who remembered. What must it be like for her living in this world? Talya felt guilty again at the comfort which she enjoyed on Silk Road. What could she do, what could any of them do? Harry couldn't cross to Silk Road, it was forbidden, there was only limited help that Talya or anybody else could give. She had Lucy to think of too, she couldn't just sacrifice her life of privilege on a principle. Could she? Talya was becoming uncertain, she felt as if she was damned whatever she did.

Wiz entered the apartment carrying supplies. He was sweaty and out of breath – he'd probably run up the stairs in half the time it had taken Talya. He seemed more cheerful than he should be, given his life in The Climbs. He was so tall too, he towered over her. She wondered how he'd ever managed to get to that height on the rations that he would be restricted to. More guilt. Talya knew she'd have to fight this, it wasn't productive.

'I got what you needed,' Wiz began, then screwed up his face at the bloodied body of Harry lying on the ground. He was choked up seeing her like that. Talya spotted it and cursed his compassion, knowing that it might be that same impulse that could cause Joe and Lucy to lose their lives in The Grid. They were good kids, but they needed to toughen up. Talya helped him out and gave him something to do.

'Hand me those bandages, Wiz. I need you to do something else for me – are you okay?'

'No problem,' said Wiz, composing himself. 'Whatever you need.'

'I want you to see Jena Parsons and see if you can get her over here to take care of Harry. She should come with Dillon. Dillon will have to act as a runner with Joe away. Jena needs to understand what's going on Wiz, she can't just hide from this. If she does, she'll lose Joe.'

The silence hung for a few moments, but Talya didn't

let them indulge it. She signaled to Wiz that he should leave by beginning to attend to Harry's wounds, and he was off, as quickly as he'd arrived.

As soon as she'd taken care of Harry she was going to make that house call on Max Penner.

Summoned

Mitchell walked through the gates, the open top of his bag showing the fresh produce that it contained. He went unchallenged, the Centuria just considered it another futile charity trip from a hopeless do-gooder. Had they taken more trouble to search the bag, they'd have seen a vast array of tech. This type of equipment did not belong in The Climbs, there could be no possible use for it here. Mitchell's contraband went through unchallenged. He only began to breathe again once he was out of sight of the gates.

He had to think where to go to get to Harriet's block. He was most used to visiting Joe, but he kept out of The Climbs if he could. It was only because of Lucy that he'd got involved – any chance to be near her. He envied Joe's easiness with her, they were like brother and sister together, he couldn't match that familiarity.

It took him a while to get on track. He found Joe's block first, then traced his steps from there. Once you'd seen one block, you'd seen them all. They called them apartments, but many of the blocks had been office space before the plague. In the desperate rush for survival that had followed, people had carved them up, creating their own territory. The word 'apartment' was an affectation from the past, few residents in The Climbs knew what it meant.

If you'd pushed Mitchell, he probably would admit to being a bit of a snob about Joe and Wiz. Sure, he liked them, they were fabulous guys. But they both smelled. He knew they couldn't help it, water was at a premium in The Climbs. But really? How did they live with it? How did Lucy ignore it? It was as if Joe's smell was invisible to her, she seemed not to notice.

Still, he did like all of them, Hannah too, he'd never felt so welcome in a group like that. He'd always been a bit of an outsider, but they'd all welcomed him into their company, celebrated his skills with tech and ignored his awkwardness. Things were heating up too much for him now; it's why he'd made his excuses when they were in the sewer the previous night, it was all a bit too risky for him. If it wasn't for Lucy, he'd have been out weeks ago.

He was going to start looking for a way out. Of course, he wanted Lucy safely out of The Grid, but her mum was Talya Slater, surely they wouldn't let anything happen to her – would they? Mitchell started the long climb up the stairs to Harry's place. This was another thing he hated about The Climbs, all those levels. Why couldn't they get power over there and fix the elevators? Everything worked fine on Silk Road. That's when the prejudice reared its head, just for a moment. That feeling in Mitchell that these people had brought this upon themselves, they were living in their own mess.

Mitchell was not accustomed to making his way up so many stairs. He was exhausted by the time he reached Harry's floor. He was sweating and his clothes were wet, his face red and puffy. Jena Parsons was there, he hadn't expected that. He'd never heard her utter a word ever since he'd known Joe. Dillon, was there too, as was Wiz, who greeted him straight away. No sign of Talya, she must have left them to it.

'How's Harry?' asked Mitchell, handing the bag to Wiz.

Wiz was more interested in the bag and its hi-tech contents. He opened it as if it were Christmas Day, discarding the fruit, bread and salted meats as if they were of no importance whatsoever. Everything he needed was there – he wished that he lived on Silk Road and he could get easy access to kit like this, just like Mitchell.

'I'm going down in the sewer this evening,' said Wiz. 'Need to get this locked into that second feed and see what's going on – you coming?'

That's just what Mitchell was hoping he wouldn't ask.

'I can't tonight, Wiz. Sorry. I need to stay at home and mind my sister.'

He could see the disappointment on Wiz's face and felt he'd need to throw in a consolation prize.

'I'll be connected at home, though. Let's set up a secure channel before I go so we can talk, I'll help out if I can.'

Wiz wasn't looking forward to negotiating that sewer on his own. He was far too tall to be down there – at the outset they'd agreed that Joe and Mitchell should do it. Mitchell had refused on the grounds of the smell, but Lucy had leapt in there anyway and offered to support Joe. She knew that rats would be the issue for Joe, she'd encountered that problem before. Wiz considered getting Dillon involved but thought better of it. Jena was in a big enough fix already without losing another member of her family.

Harry gave a loud wheeze as she sat up without warning. Jena calmed her and laid her back down on her bedding. It was getting late in the day, the trial would begin at 20:00. Mitchell needed to be back before Segregation. He made link-up arrangements with Wiz, exchanged a few words with Jena and Dillon, then started to make his way down the steps.

He hoped that Wiz hadn't seen through his lies. He

wasn't looking after his sister that night. After he had passed back through the security gates, he'd got an important meeting to attend. He'd been summoned by President Josh Delman to meet at his private apartment block in the government buildings. Apparently he was keen to seek Mitchell's expertise on a technical matter.

CHAPTER TWELVE

18:37 Screens

The screens were running pre-trial showreels in the run up to everything getting underway at 20.00. Trial beginnings always drew an audience, however small, in many cases it was the only chance to relocate loved ones who'd gone missing or been taken off by the Centuria without warning. Prison visits were not allowed by Fortrillium – when somebody disappeared on a legal charge, that was the end of it, unless they wound up in The Grid. The watching audience never knew whether to be pleased or horrified if family members or friends were involved in the latest trial. On the one hand, it meant that they could see them at last, find out what had happened and get a glimpse of them. But every time it resulted in certain death.

'Justice is seen to be done in The Grid!' boomed a voice from the screens.

The Climbs was dominated by the sound of the screens. Even those who had stayed in their apartments, or were confined to them, couldn't avoid the commentary, it permeated the blocks. On Silk Road, people watched the screens from the comfort of their homes, grateful to be reminded how lucky they were. It was rare for a Silk Roader to end up in The Grid, most knew to keep their heads down and hang on to what they'd got. The showreels were making a big deal of a bearded man called Ross, a Silk Roader, a 'violent, aggressive individual who fought with his office co-workers and injured many'. There were interviews and sound bites from so-called colleagues describing his 'mad rampage' and his 'psychological imbalances' and the camera lingered on images of the man whose arms he'd broken.

The crowds were introduced to Miron, the 'fire devil' who'd created a hellish inferno in The Climbs, burning innocent victims without mercy. There was Marjani, the child killer, who'd murdered her own daughter and killed two Centuria when trying to escape a routine check by the authorities. There was 'Rampage' – he wasn't given a proper name – a man who was shown on the screens going crazy in his cage. Most people flinched at his uninhibited aggression, but some on Silk Road were excited by the prospect of having such unbridled madness in the trial. In the crowd, a mother and father held on to each other, with tears in their eyes. They recognized 'Rampage' as their son, Chris, who'd experienced psychological troubles as a teenager and who'd been forcibly removed to the Institute three months earlier.

There were others profiled too, twelve in all in this trial, but two of the Justice Seekers had their names kept secret – they were not going to be revealed until they stepped into The Grid. There was a buzz throughout The Climbs when identities were withheld; it usually meant a celebrity, high-ranking official or other big catch for Fortrillium. The scene was set. The Justice Seekers had been introduced, the glossy showreels and booming voice-overs gripped the attention of the entire city. This was going to be a trial on a scale never seen before.

'Let justice be seen to be done!' boomed the presenter. 'It's the way of The City, an eye for an eye, a tooth for a tooth, a life for a life.'

18:52 Confined

Wiz cursed Mitchell for not accompanying him to the sewer. He was going to have a devil of a job crawling along to where they'd hacked into the networks. He'd have to enter from a different point for starters – there were Centuria guarding the entrance that they'd used previously. That meant a long cramped journey carrying a bag full of technical kit in a narrow, stinking sewer. The commentary from the screens made him keep moving on, in spite of his reluctance.

He knew who the two secret Justice Seekers were. It had to be Joe and Lucy, and stuck in The Grid they'd have to rely on their own wits and any help they could get from outside. That meant him and Mitchell, though Mitchell was probably going to be no use at all. Wiz reached the sewer entrance, put his bag on the ground, lifted the cover and manoeuvred himself awkwardly into the narrow pipeline. At least Mitchell had brought him a flashlight. Batteries were a rare thing in The Climbs, they'd have fetched him a lot of currency on the black market.

Wiz took care to replace the sewer cover and began to make his way along the dripping pipeline. He didn't share Joe's hatred of rats, which was a good job. He'd disturbed a large colony as he dropped down from the opening, and just had to stand there while they ran over his feet, fleeing the area. Wiz moved on. The flashlight was good, it would have helped Joe and Lucy on their previous visits.

He stayed alert. As far as he'd been able to tell, the Centuria were only guarding the outside of the sewer, they hadn't left it open. They were sure to have a camera down there, but Mitchell had provided him with a jammer to sort that problem out. At least there was one good thing about the tunnel, he thought. They'd just be able to replay a short extract of the video feed and nobody would ever notice – little changed down there. If he put audio on a loop too, he'd be safe to come and go, though he hoped he would not need to be back there for some time.

Mitchell had done an excellent job providing tech, at least. Wiz would be able to set up network access remotely, hopping a signal wirelessly over to Harry's apartment. He assumed the range would be enough, there was a lot standing between the sewer and the tower block. He'd got a booster and a solar charger – with no power in The Climbs he'd rely on that to stay powered up. With any luck, every-thing would work and he'd be able to remain in hiding in the high-rise. He'd taken a risk coming out, but he'd kept alert and managed to avoid any Centuria so far. It didn't take long before his back began to ache. He cursed his height but pressed on regardless.

Wiz found it difficult to work out exactly where he was. He'd remembered that it was two right turns and a left. As he made the left turn he became more alert, taking care to be as quiet as he could. He was sure there would be no guards in the sewer, there was only so long you could stay down there, but he would have been amazed if they hadn't used cameras. Sure enough, as he began to make the left turn, he caught the reflection of a green flickering light. A NightCam – he immediately recognized the distinctive colour, this was Centuria standard issue. A piece of luck at last, he could break into this quickly enough.

Wiz ducked back around the corner of the sewer and quietly drew out a console. He activated a search, found three NightCam IDs in the immediate area, then accessed each remotely via a secure link. He waited patiently for two minutes as he recorded a video and sound loop, then he sent his recordings directly to the output channels. He did a double check to make sure there were no more cameras and that the loops were working, then he moved on.

He made straight for the opening where Lucy and Joe had left the network cables. He could see signs of disturbance, Fortrillium had sent their own tech team down there. A second lucky break, they hadn't sealed the area yet. He'd be able to insert the ReRouters into the wires and they'd never know. The RRs as they were known entered each individual wire, sending the data carried wirelessly to a separate unit, encrypting it and only reassembling in a readable form when it reached a suitably adapted console – in this case, the one that Wiz was carrying at that moment. The RRs were Fortrillium manufactured – without Mitchell they never could have got their hands on them – and for that reason Wiz hoped they'd sit undetected in the cables.

Wiz ran his checks. Two streams, one from Fortrillium, one from the second source. Who knew where that one went? The Fortrillium source fed through correctly, and Wiz was able to access the secure area which Matt Parson's data card had unlocked. So far, so good. Mitchell had created a protocol for the second feed. They were shooting in the dark because it wasn't in a format that they were used to. The feed came through – a graph on Wiz's console opened up, showing there was data running on the line that moment. Interesting, they'd only detected it before at the end of the last trial, yet here it was, active, before the latest trial had even begun.

Wiz checked the time – still just under one hour to go until the trial. He tried a few routines to unscramble the flow but had no luck. He confirmed the information on his console for a second time, realizing his mistake. It was audio data running along the line, he'd need speaker output to hear what was going on.

He routed in an audio output, but only a scrambled sound came out, it was meaningless. Wiz took an extract and ran it through a reassembling program. It wasn't perfect, but he could just about make it out.

He recognized the voice immediately. It wasn't so much the voice as the speed and delivery. He'd been listening to it for the past hour, booming through the screens, reminding citizens in The City what a transparent justice system they all enjoyed.

'Let justice be seen to be done!' he'd declared on one of the showreels.

It was President Josh Delman. He was speaking to somebody outside The City's walls.

19:06 Encounter

Talya had not been entirely happy about leaving Harry with Jena, but she needed to move fast. Jena had at least shaken herself out of her usual trance enough to attend to Harry's wounds. She had to get to Max Penner, he'd be finishing his shift and on his way to his home soon. Fortrillium usually changed shifts at 19:00, they were long days. She was running a bit late, she hoped he wouldn't be delayed because of the trial.

She thought she'd missed him, arriving at the gated entrance to Fortrillium a little later than she'd have liked. As she'd turned away from the gates in frustration, she'd just caught sight of Max in the distance. She started to jog, but it quickly turned into a run. Her legs were aching badly from the trial of having to walk up to Harry's apartment, but she pushed through the pain, determined to get to Max away from the intimidation of the Centuria.

Max became aware of fast approaching footsteps, instinctively sensing that they were heading towards him. It took him a split second to recognize Talya – he saw the face then made the connection. He was immediately defensive and continued walking as they spoke.

'Mr Penner,' she began, thinking that formal and respectful might be the best approach.

'Law Lord Slater,' he replied. 'What a coincidence seeing you so soon after your visit!'

Max knew that this was no fluke, he'd seen enough of the trial build-up on his own screen at work to know what had happened since he'd last seen Talya. Her face was desperate. Of course it was, the trial began in under an hour. But he couldn't help.

'You know about my daughter I assume?'

'I do, I'm sorry.'

'Is there any way to get into The Grid area from where you work, do you ever go in yourself?'

'I'm forbidden to talk to anybody about my job, other than under strict supervision—'

'Enough of that, Mr Penner. Do you have family?'

Max didn't, he felt as if it was best not to have too many close connections in The City. He shook his head.

'My daughter enters that place at 20:00 and I need to

do whatever I can to keep her alive. You work there, Mr Penner, there must be a way in!'

'You can't get in, only the bots enter and leave, they take care of all the maintenance and the cleaning.'

'If the bots can get in, so can a human,' Talya began, but Max held up his hand to stop her going on.

'If any living creature enters those tunnel areas, they're burned to a crisp. Nothing living goes in or out of there unless they're part of a trial. There's one way in and one way out, and I've never seen the way out used in my lifetime.'

Talya hadn't either, nobody had. She wasn't giving up.

'Can equipment be sent through with the bots, communicators or anything like that?'

Max knew where she was going with this. He liked Talya Slater, but he also liked living. He'd risked enough sending the WristCom in, he wasn't in a hurry to get involved in any of Talya's plans. She was on a suicide mission, Law Lord or not.

'That's impossible too, everything that goes in and out is screened.' A lie, yes, but it would make her go away.

Talya's tone changed, he sensed it immediately. She was done with pushing against a closed door.

'Mr Penner, why was my husband's WristCom sitting on your desk earlier? I think the Centuria might like to know about that.'

He was immediately on the defensive, he cursed himself for not having concealed it better. Max quickly ran through his options in his head. Should he come clean? Or help this woman who was trying to lean on him and threaten him? Perhaps she would offer some protection?

He did the only thing that he could.

'I'm sorry, Law Lord Slater, I can't talk to you now, I have to go.'

Max rushed towards his front door which was now only yards away and locked himself in securely.

19:23 Prepped

Joe was thrown back into the cell area. Clay and Lucy rushed to see how he was. They'd taken some time to come round, though Clay still had a terrible ache in his brain – he'd never experienced anything like it. Psyche-Eval is what they'd called it. He'd never known something so painful and he'd had a few knocks and bruises in his time, including the pounding he'd taken during his sentencing before the Law Lords.

The Psyche-Eval devices entered the brain via their noses. Their heads had been restrained in braces, no anaesthetic was offered, and it hurt. Two large tubes moved to the top of their nostrils, and then from within them two tiny needles went directly into the brain. The pain was sudden, sharp and intense, but was quickly replaced by a mild pulse, which seemed like a dark, leaden fog in the mind. Several of the inmates screamed out at this stage, the sensation was excruciating but mercifully brief.

One of the medical team who had administered this procedure seemed more talkative than the others. Piecing together what had happened in the cell, Clay, Lucy and Marjani had worked out they were looking for fears, phobias and life events. No explanation was given as to why, but they knew that bit already. They'd all seen enough of the trials to work it out. Many of the scenarios inside The Grid would be based on personal experiences and terrors. As somebody watching on the screens, it wasn't clear how those had come into play. They understood now, though. They'd be teased and tormented with their greatest fears when the trial began. For the moment they focused on Joe. There was an unspoken agreement that they needed to stay sharp and calm.

They'd caught a fleeting glimpse of the person in the next cell to them. He was only young, clearly distressed, but receiving no comfort at all, just constant contempt from the guards. They'd do what they could to help him inside The Grid, they'd try to keep an eye out for him, but they doubted that he'd survive long, whatever they did.

Joe was feeling the impact of two tranquilizers and a Psyche-Eval. His chest was red raw from the punishment he'd received earlier, the flesh sore and bloody still, his brain pounding from what had just taken place in the medical area.

'Hell, my head hurts!'

'Mine too,' said Clay. 'The others don't seem too bad.'

'What were they doing in there? It was horrible, did you hear me calling out?'

Nobody had heard Joe scream, not that it would have mattered, there was no victory in managing to keep silent, there was no need for bravado. They were all terrified, but they would only survive if they could master their fear. That would be a battle fought alone and in silence in the hours that lay ahead.

Joe needed a moment to sit down and get his mind back on track. Whatever had been done to him in there, it felt as if his thoughts had been scrambled and they were just starting to settle down and re-order themselves.

'We need to plan, we need to think about how it starts,' Clay began.

'There's always something horrible at the beginning,' Miron added. 'They always go for shock value.'

'How many of us in the trial? Did anybody manage to count?' asked Lucy.

'At least ten, I think,' said Joe, who'd been last to go for the Psyche-Eval. 'There's another cell. I counted four more – and the person next to us. They'll pick someone off early, they always do in the first ten minutes.'

Lucy had seen more trials than she'd have liked. She would force herself to watch at times, it was too easy to turn away and pretend it wasn't happening. She wanted to stare the horror in the face; by doing that she felt that she was honouring those in the trial. Turning away or treating it as entertainment denied the atrocities which they all acquiesced in. She would not look away. It was how Joe's father had died, after all.

The time for talk was over. Joe had barely recovered enough to walk properly.

Heavily armed escorts had arrived – the inmates were to be shackled together by the ankles. The neck devices were removed. There were more guards than prisoners; something serious was happening next, they appeared to be expecting runners.

'What's going on?' asked Clay, hoping he'd not be rewarded by a burst of the electronic batons.

'Your trial begins in twenty minutes,' answered one of the guards. 'We're taking you to The Grid.'

19:37 First Blood

Hannah was feeling nervous. Nobody knew how these trials worked, but she hadn't expected to go into lock-down when the trial was confirmed. No entrance or exit was permitted until there were no Justice Seekers left standing. Or, they got a Justice Walk by surviving.

A large clock had gone live in the work area; it was counting down until the trial began. Hannah hadn't a clue that her friends were involved – things had moved so fast since the competition that she'd had no time to catch up with Lucy. Where was Lucy? Why hadn't she been in contact? Hannah's WristCom was disabled now, it had been blocked the minute the trial confirmation came through. She was cut off until the trial was over. It was contempt of court for her to discuss an ongoing trial.

There was no showreel playing either. The Gridders were given no knowledge of the Justice Seekers, only their profiles and gender.

97TRaider sidled up to Hannah, he had something to share with her. He was proving a useful source of information.

'They're going to first blood you,' he whispered. 'Have something up your sleeve. It's an initiation test.'

Hannah's first reaction was to panic, but she quickly calmed herself. She'd asked for this, this was her chance to find out what went on in the trials. Lucy and Joe could use this information, they might finally be able to bring down Fortrillium with what she was learning here.

97TRaider sensed her question.

'They'll give you first kill, but it'll have to be good. They like drama to begin the trials. Get thinking, they'll tell you with fifteen minutes to go, it won't play well if you don't come up with something.'

Hannah moved back to her work area and began rendering a play environment on the screen. Texture, depth, temperature, sound – she was able to control everything by the touch of a button and the selection of a menu. A new message arrived at the top of her main screen. She opened it up. It was about the Psyche-Evals. The profiles were being downloaded to the primary database, they'd need those later as the trial developed.

The Head Gridder called for everybody's attention, they were entering the final minutes now. Hannah figured this would be the pep talk, the motivational chat before the killing began. She had to get over that. The carnage would go on anyway – with or without her. She was there to try and bring an end to it. Lucy, Joe, Mitchell and Wiz, if they could, they were going to stop this brutality.

'We have sixteen minutes until entry,' she began. 'The selection is taking place now, we'll know how many Modes in the next five minutes. We have a new member of the team with us today, and because of that we're giving Janexx2 first-blood privileges. Janexx2, get to work and make it something powerful to open with.'

Hannah was still adjusting to being referred to by her gaming name – it was how anonymity was preserved for the Gridders beyond Fortrillium's walls. They became celebrated figures on the screens, but nobody ever knew who the Gridders were, identities were shrouded in secrecy.

'Mr Hunter has sent me a personal memo insisting that we make this trial special. You need to make the gameplay powerful, he's promised a cull if we fail to reach an engagement score of less than 9.1. You know what you have to do, everybody!'

They were dismissed. Hannah didn't like the sound of a cull but she was familiar with engagement scores, it was how they measured attentiveness to a trial. Damien Hunter wanted The City gripped with this trial, and a score of 9.1 would ensure that everybody was talking about it.

She put any thoughts about a cull to the back of her

mind, she had her own challenge to meet and a deadline coming up fast behind her.

Hannah became Janexx2 and set to work on her gameplay. She had to forget that these were human beings. On their screens they'd just see digitally rendered figures, they never got to see the real action. She typed at her console and worked hard to concentrate on the challenge. She'd have to sacrifice these Justice Seekers, but their deaths would count for something. With what she would learn at Fortrillium, she was sure they could eventually stop the senseless killing.

So Hannah mastered her conscience and set about the task in hand. The first kill would be hers. And it would take their breath away.

19:42 Scream

Jena stroked the hair away from Harry's eyes; she was still semi-conscious but had become increasingly restless. Most of the blood had been cleared away from the wounds and Jena had utilized the few dressings that Wiz had managed to find to cover them as best she could. Clean bandages were hard to get your hands on in The Climbs – these didn't seem to be new, but they weren't too dirty at least.

As Jena sat there, she listened to the muffled boom from the screens outside. They were high up, the sound wasn't clear, but she knew what was going on.

She'd been here before. Dillon and Joe were much younger then, and she'd just collapsed at the time. Every day she tried to will herself on, she saw how much of the load that Joe was carrying, but she'd just crumpled when Matt died. She was perpetually frightened, terrified of what might happen at any moment, paralysed at the thought of taking action. She knew it was ridiculous, but she was imprisoned by her own mind, she just couldn't master it.

So she cowered, seldom leaving the house, never speaking to anybody, locked up in the prison of her own fear. She'd known that Joe was in trouble, she'd understood what they'd said to her, but she just wanted to fold in on herself and disappear. If she could have killed herself, she would have, but she was too terrified even to do that.

It was checkmate in a game that only she was playing, there was no move for her to make, just existing, marking the hours, a captive in her own life.

When Wiz had come to the apartment it had stirred her, she'd sensed his urgency, understood the seriousness of what was going on. She'd grasped that Joe was in trouble, it was happening again. Joe, wonderful Joe, who'd kept them all alive since Matt was taken away.

She owed him this at least. She felt harnessed to her own fears, but she forced herself to stand up and leave the apartment with Wiz. Every step was painful, her mind was filled with a thousand horrors, but she willed herself on. Surely anything would be better than the living death that she'd inflicted on herself for six years? If she was ever going to change things, now was the time. If Joe died, they'd both perish, Dillon was still too young to do what Joe had done. He was different to Joe, he didn't have that determination. The same determination that had got Matt killed.

Harry was getting restless, she was mouthing words now, her eyes still closed, but her body jumping about as if it was possessed.

'Delman ... must tell Talya ... President Delman ...'

Jena could just make the words out. She put her ear to the old woman's lips, struggling to hear what she was trying to say.

'It was Delman ... I remember now ... he was alive, how could he be alive?'

Jena stroked Harry's hair, trying to calm her down, but desperate to grasp some meaning from her words. Harry made one last effort to pass on the memory which had been troubling her. It would cost her her life. Harry's body went still and limp, but her deadly secret had passed into the world on her final breath.

'Delman, he was there before the plague ... he was part of it ... Delman could have prevented the disease.'

19:51 Hidden

Damien Hunter loved the stillness of the Umbilica, even though it held so much sadness for him. He always went there before a trial, it reminded him of the purpose of his struggles. He reached out and touched his daughter through the transparent film. He could feel her tiny heart beating. He dreamed of being able to hold her hands for real one day and have her running alongside him, with his son calling out behind.

And there was his beautiful wife Cassie, how he longed to hold her again and hear her laughter. Her body twitched as if she knew he was there, but that was impossible, her sleep was deep, he had to walk this path alone.

He dreamed of having them all at his side again, to experience the pure happiness of family. But that was not his lot. It nourished him to be in there, alone with them, away from the fear and expectation of those who were cowed by him in The City.

He studied the innocent, white faces of his beautiful children and touched the outstretched hand of his wife.

'It's close now,' he told them. 'We're nearly there, we'll be together again soon.'

He closed his eyes, took a deep breath and stared ahead.

It was almost 20:00. He would need to open the trial. If Slater came, he'd be amazed, but she was tough, she'd keep fighting him until the end.

'I'll see you shortly,' he whispered to Cassie. 'I love you.'

Damien Hunter wiped the tear from his eye and made himself stand tall. There was killing to be done. Lives had to be ended if he was ever going to hold his family again, and he would stop at nothing to achieve that goal.

19:58 Sentenced

There were twelve of them in all, they hadn't known the final numbers until the last minute. They were in a dark room, shackled in a circle and facing outward. There was complete silence except for the man that they'd seen earlier; he was sobbing and weeping as if he was able to understand what was about to happen.

'Lucy, Clay, you there?' asked Joe. They'd been split up just before the end, it was disorienting, he was sure they were still there.

'I'm here,' said Lucy, 'Miron and Marjani too.'

'When it begins, stay together,' said Clay. 'Whoever you are, whatever you did, stay close – we fight as a unit and we survive.'

'Screw you!' came a voice. It was unfamiliar, nobody who'd been in their cell.

The room lit up, it was complete darkness all around them, but they could see each other.

Joe counted up fast. There was Ross and the woman from

their cage who hadn't wanted to get involved – she was wearing white overalls, the same as two others, both men. Smugglers, three of them. If they came from The Climbs, smuggling was all about survival, that was all. Joe did it every day.

There was one yellow overall. That was somebody from the Institute, he was sobbing. That must have been the man in the cell next to them.

He was moving around the circle quickly now – one more set of orange overalls, a woman, assault, same as Ross.

It was the black overalls that bothered him. You seldom saw black in The Grid. It had come from the man who'd cursed Clay moments earlier. A serial killer, a great hate figure for the people watching on the screens. Everybody loathed a serial killer, it was the type of crime for which there was never any excuse, no decent explanation.

A voice boomed from all around them. They knew this well, it was the beginning of the trial. The voice was Damien Hunter's.

'An eye for an eye, a tooth for a tooth, a life for a life. So it is in our city that any person who breaks the law shall find justice in The Grid. It has been our way since the plague years, it has kept our city safe and fair for almost one hundred years.'

Joe noticed how the lighting had left their feet in shadow. He'd never seen shackles before and had wondered why the Justice Seekers never ran. They'd concealed them in the darkness so that the cameras didn't pick them up. The voice began again.

'Thirteen Justice Seekers will enter The Grid today. If any find justice there, they will walk away with their freedom. This is how our society preserves truth and honesty.'

Joe surveyed the circle, counting the figures on the platform once more. He counted twelve again. Who was the thirteenth? Where was the thirteenth?

The lights moved to an area behind the Justice Seekers, illuminating six Law Lords who were projected as holographic images. They stood there in a line, in their black legal gowns. The trial would begin with the dropping of Leianna Richwald's gavel.

Damien Hunter's voice was replaced by Leianna Richwald's.

'You thirteen stand charged with crimes against The City. If you find justice in The Grid, you shall walk free.'

Where was the thirteenth? Joe didn't like it, they were up to something.

'Law Lord Sivil will now determine the Modes.'

A number was drawn out of a small black bag. Sivil held it up for the Justice Seekers to see.

'There shall be three Modes in the first hearing.'

Joe wasn't sure if he should be relieved or not. It could have been better – two Modes – but it could have been a lot worse, five, seven or even nine perhaps. The fewer the Modes, the greater the chance of making it through to the final trial. However many Modes, they were probably all going to die, unless Hannah, Wiz and Mitchell were working on a plan.

'Justice Seekers, you may enter The Grid. Find your justice!'

Hunter's voice boomed once again, the lights went out, and the Law Lords could no longer be seen.

Joe felt the shackles release around his ankles. All twelve on the platform scrutinized the area, waiting for the first threat that would come to take their lives.

20:00 The Grid

The Climbs was alive with the anticipation of the new trial. Most could barely watch, the first minutes always began with a death. As the commentary boomed throughout the tower blocks, Jena finally let go of Harry's hand. Many memories would die with the demise of this remarkable woman, but before she had passed from the wicked world in which she lived, she had managed to pass on a final memory to those who survived. It would eventually reveal the dark truth that had been hiding in The City. Jena covered Harry's body with a dirty, ragged sheet and signaled to Dillon. They intended to work with Talya, they were going to help to save Joe.

At the same time as Jena was leaving the old woman's sorry corpse, President Josh Delman was shaking Mitchell's hand and welcoming him into his imposing office. Mitchell wasn't entirely sure why he'd been summoned, but within the next fifteen minutes he would accept an offer from the President and betray his friends.

Elsewhere in The Climbs, Wiz typed frantically at his console in the damp darkness, cleaning up the audio from The City's President. He'd stumbled on something that could save his companions – but condemn Josh Delman to be a hunted man.

Talya Slater hadn't bothered to turn up for the beginning of the trial, she'd decided to spend her time more productively, whatever the consequences for her. After being hastily dismissed by Max Penner, she'd gone to the back of his house, kicked down his door and confronted him in his kitchen. At the time her daughter's trial began, Talya was twisting a carving knife which she'd plunged into Max's hand to encourage him to share a little more willingly. Max would not hang out for long before he fainted and the knife tore through his flesh as he fell to the ground. Before he hit the floor, he would have given Talya a glimpse of hope, the possibility that lives could be saved.

Damien Hunter had retired to the solitude of the Umbilica, where he was holding his wife's hand through the protective film once again. He always became emotional during the trials – each one offered him the promise of reclaiming his family.

Hannah checked her console, her Gridder colleagues were all focused on the large screen at the front of the room, where the digitized events in The Grid would play out before them. Hannah didn't know that Joe and Lucy were in there. She'd prepared a spectacle that could kill two of the people who were closest to her.

'Are you ready?' asked the Head Gridder. Hannah nodded. She had to do this. She knew it was wrong, but they had to take lives to save lives.

Hannah began the trial. Everything changed around the Justice Seekers as a new environment rendered. There was a roar of flames, the heat was intense. The Justice Seekers were caught in the middle, there seemed no way to escape. Then Joe saw movement within the fire, there was somebody in there already, he couldn't make it out at first.

It had to be the thirteenth Justice Seeker, the one that nobody had seen yet. There was a cry from Chris, it was animal-like in its rawness, he was scared for his life, he didn't know what to do.

Whoever was in the flames moved awkwardly towards the centre where the Justice Seekers were trapped. The badly burned body fell at Joe's feet. No wonder the movement had seemed unusual, the thirteenth man was that day's first victim of The Grid.

It was Zach Fuller. They'd given him crutches, but the charred body was his. They'd put him in there so that Joe could see his friend burned alive. The first Justice Seeker had fallen inside The Grid.

As Joe held Zach's scorched hand, the life slipped away from his friend. Joe vowed that he would be delivering his own justice to Damien Hunter, and when it came it would be merciless and final.

PREVIEW FROM THE GRID 2

Killer

Already their numbers were depleted, but he knew he was safe, until the end at least. Sure, his crimes were ugly, but that made him useful inside The Grid. He didn't know who'd had the idea, but even though he was probably going to perish with the rest of them, it was inspired. The audiences watching on the screens would love it, he'd die a celebrity, even though they'd all despise him. What better way to exit this hellhole – as the most reviled man in The City?

He'd had a good run. Few people cared what went on in The Climbs; if there was a murder here or an assault there, nobody in power bothered. The majority of arrests were politically motivated, and that had left him free to do whatever he wanted, to whomever he wanted.

They called him a serial killer, but there was much more to it than that. He hated the word killer, he considered himself more of an artist. Every person he'd ever killed had been like painting a picture, it was a multi-layered thing.

Starting with the idea, the rough sketch, then building up the layers, step by step.

The word killer made what he did sound commonplace or ordinary. What he did to his victims was far from ordinary. His unique skill was in drawing out the moment of death. It fascinated him how much of the body you could actually remove and still keep a person alive, in sustained terror and pain. He'd have to improvise a little in The Grid, they could not provide him with his usual tools, not straight away, but he'd been told to make his first move as soon as possible.

The survivors from the fireball were tired and exhausted after their first challenge. They were in need of rest before the trial continued. They'd have to use the daytime to find food and shelter, plan their defence and prepare for what came next. They were never safe, but the best trials came in the evenings when more people were gripped by what was playing out on the screens.

Now they thought they'd reached sanctuary, for a short time at least; he'd make his first move and break off from the primary group. So far, they were sticking together, but if past trials were anything to go by, they'd be split up within the first twenty-four hours and pitted against each other.

He surveyed those who were left and wondered who he would pick as his first victim. This was the artist in him, a regular killer would not be so fussy. Then the decision was made for him. One of the women was getting up to explore the woodland environment in which they'd recently been placed inside The Grid. Lots of cover and places to hide, just how he liked it. This would be his first masterpiece. He'd conceal her somewhere safe where he could work on her deliberately, allowing her to savour every one of her final minutes as he killed her, slowly, painfully, over a number of hours. They'd never even guess what was going on.

This wasn't killing, this was artistry. And who better to target for his first masterpiece? As Lucy got up quietly to scout around for food, he followed behind, excited and exhilarated that his first kill would come so soon.

Message

Wiz typed fast at his console. He was so close, but they were onto him, there was no time left. If only he'd realized what Matt had done sooner, they'd have had more time to work with the information. Matt had had to make it secure, of course he had, and he must have had a lot of faith in Joe to think that he'd finally be able to crack the encryption.

Well, Joe was gone, it was up to him. He'd seen them enter the building moments before, looking down from Harry's apartment. How long would it take them to reach him? They wouldn't move as fast as Wiz could, they had equipment to carry, those black suits to wear. He had ten minutes surely, maybe even as many as fifteen if he got lucky. He'd never considered having no elevators a blessing, but that day he was grateful that everybody had to use the stairs, it might save some lives. If he could just see what Matt had left them and send it over to Talya, it wouldn't matter so much if they got him now. Talya would be able to take it from there if it came to that.

He kept entering the codes, cursing that Mitchell had betrayed his whereabouts. What had he been offered in return? What had made it worth forsaking his companions and sending them to almost certain death? Wiz hoped that Mitchell could live with himself after this, he thought they'd been friends. He'd been sure they were friends.

Every time he entered a new password, an obstructing beep would sound on his console, denying him access. He pictured the staircase, trying to assess how far the Centuria would have made it by now. Level 10 maybe, Level 15 at the most, and there was debris at Level 17 that slowed everybody down.

Then there was a different sound, he almost missed it, he was so used to being blocked. His console began to run a program, it was like nothing he'd ever seen before, he wasn't sure what was happening. It took about half a minute. The device drew what little solar power it had managed to store in Harry's apartment and, like a ghost from another world, a holographic image of Matt appeared in front on him.

Wiz had never known Matt personally, his death was before he'd even met Joe, but he realized who it was anyway, there was only one person it could be. He wished Joe could see this – he knew how much he'd have liked to see his own father again.

The holographic image was unstable, and Matt had taken a few moments before he'd begun to record his message. The projected image of Joe's dead father started to speak. Wiz heard the smashing of debris from the stairwell out on the landing, they'd reached Level 17. He hoped he'd have enough time to catch the message.

'Joe, if you're watching this you've turned into the man I knew you'd become. I'm so sorry about what happened, but when I tell you what was going on, you'll understand why I did what I had to do. Joe, I wish I could be with you, it was the hardest thing I've ever had to do in my life to leave you, Dillon and Jena. But if you're watching this now, it could soon be over. You must never let Fortrillium know about this Joe, whatever they try to do to you. If they know what

I'm about to tell you it will all be over. Joe, I know this will be difficult for you but ...'

The holographic image of Matt hesitated, he seemed to be a man who had a lot on his mind. He stared directly into Wiz's eyes, it was almost as if he was there. The sound of heavy boots could be heard thundering up the stairwell, there wasn't much time now.

'Joe, this will be difficult to believe, but you have to trust me. I know what you saw on the screens, I know what everybody saw. But the truth is Joe, it was all a deception. I'm still alive Joe and you need to come to me as soon as you can ...'

The story continues in The Grid 2: Quest For Vengeance.

ABOUT THE AUTHOR

Hi, I'm Paul Teague, the author of The Secret Bunker Trilogy and The Grid Trilogy as well as several other psychological thrillers and non-fiction titles.

I'm a former broadcaster and journalist with the BBC, but I have also worked as a primary school teacher, a disc jockey, a shopkeeper, a waiter and a sales rep.

I've loved sci-fi all of my life, starting with the Danny Dunn books and progressing to the huge franchises such as Terminator, Star Trek, Babylon 5, The Hunger Games and The Maze Runner series.

Be first to hear about new books and special offers:
https://paulteague.net

www.ingramcontent.com/pod-product-compliance
Lightning Source LLC
Chambersburg PA
CBHW021333190726
48288CB00003B/1095